LOVE 'EM AND LEAVE 'EM

Drusilla slipped the chemise up over her head, shook her dark hair loose and walked toward Shelter. She made a soft cat-like purr as he kissed the point of her chin, her naval and her breasts in turn.

His eyes went over her body as she swayed beneath him. Her breasts flattened, her abdomen was firmly muscled beneath a layer of soft, feminine flesh, and it quivered now as Shell went to his knees. Lost in pleasure, Drusilla moaned and then shuddered.

Eyes still feasting on her white, star-glossed body, Shelter trembled and shook with release. Drusilla kissed his closed eyes, holding him close, never wanting to leave his side. But as gunshots suddenly thundered from across the desert flats, she realized he would have to go—he was a stalked man, hunting another, and until he found revenge he would never love her again . . .

MORE EXCITING WESTERNS FROM ZEBRA!

THE GUNN SERIES BY JORY SHERMAN

GUNN #12: THE WIDOW-MAKER   (987, $2.25)
Gunn offers to help the lovely ladies of Luna Creek when the ruthless Widow-maker gang kills off their husbands. It's hard work, but the rewards are mounting!

GUNN #13: ARIZONA HARDCASE   (1039, $2.25)
When a crafty outlaw threatens the lives of some lovely females, Gunn's temper gets mean and hot—and he's got no choice but to shoot it off!

GUNN #14: THE BUFF RUNNERS   (1093, $2.25)
Gunn runs into two hell-raising sisters caught in the middle of a buffalo hunter's feud. He hires out his sharpshooting skills—and doubles their fun!

THE BOLT SERIES BY CORT MARTIN

BOLT #6: TOMBSTONE HONEYPOT   (1009, $2.25)
In Tombstone, Bolt meets up with luscious Honey Carberry who tricks him into her beehive. But Bolt has a stinger of his own!

BOLT #7: RAWHIDE WOMAN   (1057, $2.25)
Rawhide Kate's on the lookout for the man who killed her family. And when Bolt snatches the opportunity to come to Kate's rescue, she learns how to handle a tricky gun!

BOLT #8: HARD IN THE SADDLE   (1095, $2.25)
When masked men clean him of his cash, Bolt's left in a tight spot with a luscious lady. He pursues the gang—and enjoys a long, hard ride on the way!

Available wherever paperbacks are sold, or order direct from the Publisher. Send cover price plus 50¢ per copy for mailing and handling to Zebra Books, 475 Park Avenue South, New York, N.Y. 10016. DO NOT SEND CASH.

SHELTER

HANGING MOON #2

BY PAUL LEDD

ZEBRA BOOKS
KENSINGTON PUBLISHING CORP.

ZEBRA BOOKS

are published by

KENSINGTON PUBLISHING CORP.
475 Park Avenue South
New York, N.Y. 10016

THIRD PRINTING

Printed in the United States of America

1.

Shelter Morgan awakened to the patter of rain on the hotel roof. He stretched his long frame and slid from bed, crossing the room to the window to study the town. Leadville still slept in the gray of predawn. Bunched thunderheads raked the mountains with a steady downpour. The street below was only a bog. Dawn was a hushed flash of silver streaking the eastern skies.

It had been raining a week, ceaselessly. Morgan let the curtain fall back into place and he turned back toward the bed, the floorboards cold underfoot.

Another day would be lost, another day in which the killers might hide deeper in their holes. He frowned deeply, sagging onto the bed.

"It can't be that bad," Linda said with a smile. She sat up in the bed, her profuse blond hair in nightstrewn madness. Her breasts, full, nearly round, fell from the covering sheets like ripe fruit and Shell's hand went instantly to them as Linda bent her head to his, stroking Shell's bare back.

Shell kissed her breasts, letting his lips linger on her taut nipples as Linda ran a toying finger around the whorl of his ear.

"It's still raining," Shell whispered.

"I know it," she breathed, biting at his neck. "That means you'll be staying."

Linda smiled deeply, sensuously and her head lolled back against the pillow of Shelter Morgan's bed, her pale hair spread out across it. She lay there watching this tall, blond man, liking his deeply tanned hands and face, the cordlike muscles across his shoulders and along his thighs, those deep blue-gray eyes which could be so cold, yet sparkled with merriment at the right moment. At moments such as this . . . Linda held his head, drawing it to her breasts as she felt with a tingle of anticipation, Shell's rough hand sliding to her thigh just above her knee. Reflexively her knees went up slightly and she spread her legs, offering him sanctuary. A sudden, dizzy thrill spread across her abdomen, rising along her spine and Linda bit at Shell's neck as his mouth searched her breasts.

Her thighs were soft, silky and Shell let his hand dally there, stroking the inside of her legs, feeling a slight, anxious tremor beneath the skin.

His fingers trailed upward and played in the downy, golden hair which covered her pubic mound. Simultaneously he felt Linda's long fingers drop to his crotch. She gave a little gasp of expectation as she circled his shaft with inquisitive fingers, gently tracing patterns up and down the long erection, from the root to the sensitive head which she squeezed hard once.

Her tongue shot into Shell's mouth as her hand excitedly stroked him. Shell's own fingers had dipped into Linda, finding her warm, wet, ready. He spread her slightly, running a tantalizing finger across the sweet silk of her flesh. Slowly she rolled over to him and she took his shaft with both boths, rubbing herself on it as she panted into Shell's ear.

He slipped a hand under her, drawing her buttocks nearer as Linda spread herself and Shell felt her enveloping warmth as she slid onto him, her hands still clenching his erection.

Their fingers met there for a moment, interwined as Shell stroked her just above, then below where they joined, Linda excited by the scent and warmth of her own moistness, by the searching fingers, the rigid, pulsing shaft between her legs.

Her hands left his and went suddenly to his shoulders, her teeth biting at his muscular, down covered chest. She let her mouth search his small, hard nipples and she began swaying, thrusting at him with her hips as Shell's hands went to her buttocks, keeping her tight against him. Linda cried out, in a low, hungry voice and went rigid against him.

They lay side by side, pressed tightly together, her warm thighs against his, her breasts flattened against his chest, their lips locked together.

Linda's hair was damp wih perspiration, and she looked at Shell with green eyes which were glossed, distant, absorbing. She ground against him, a series of whispering moans rising deep in her throat.

"Come on, Baby," he told her. "Make it nice." He petted her hair, their eyes locked together. Her breasts ground against him, and now she worked her pelvis against his methodically, trancelike, he could feel her filling with moisture.

"Make it nice."

He smiled, and her lips parted in what had begun as a smile but which her sudden gush of emotion changed into an animal, open-mouthed exultation.

Linda came undone and she began a savage thrusting, her head twisting from side to side as she clawed at Shell's shoulders and back, her teeth finding his throat, chest, arms.

Her back arched and she halted suddenly, motionless. The she relaxed, a series of tiny, convulsive spasms beginning deep within her.

"Please," she murmured, "Shell." Her hair was in wild disarray, her mouth parted, tiny beads of perspiration on her upper lips as her hands kneaded Shell's shoulders. "Please . . . come for me. I want it. For me . . ." she urged him, but he needed no urging.

The ache which had begun deep in his loins had now become a driving need and as Linda's fingers reached down, touching him as he thrust against her, cradling him, he came in a hot, trembling climax.

"Yes," she murmured, breathing into his ear, letting her fingers remain on him where they joined, stroking his thighs, running a lingering finger up along the cleft between his buttocks where light, wiry hairs grew.

"Let it rain," she said out loud. "God." She lay still for a time after that, her heart pounding against his, her breath coming in ragged spurts.

Shell felt her muscles contract and he held her close while a shudder swept over her body, his lips and hers joined in a series of tiny, sucking kisses.

"Again?" he asked with a smile and she nodded slowly.

"With you it's not just once. It's a long wave, Shell. Sweeping across me. When I think it's gone . . ."

She buried her head against his chest and again Shell felt her come, and he smiled to himself, touching her lower back, her smooth buttocks, holding her near.

"I don't want it to stop raining," she said. Her mouth was twisted into a petulant pout. She had something else to say, but she fell silent, seeing immediately that Shelter Morgan did not want to discuss it.

He would go when the rains stopped. He was stalking a man, she knew, and it was that which came first. The long trail and the vengeance which lay at the end. She understood, but she did not like it. She glanced up. Shell's eyes were closed, and she kissed his eyelids softly, lying quietly beside him.

Behind those eyes the memories lived vividly, and Shell lived within them, so real were they. Slaughter, faces twisted with pain, eyes looking to him for help . . . a help he could not provide.

The memories lived . . .

The life had been wrung from the Confederacy. Sherman had cut a fiery swath across the heart of Georgia and Shell's battalion had been cut off near the Tennessee line.

And across that line, near Lookout Mountain, a withdrawing General Bragg had abandoned a cache of gold. Gold which was worth boots, medicine, ammunition, food for the ragged Southern troops.

Shell had stood before them in a smoky tent, shaking his head. "You can't mean it?"

Colonel Fainier had done most of the talking. Now he looked sharply at Shell.

"I assure you, Captain, I do mean it."

Shell kept his mouth shut. Major Twyner, the bitter, one-armed Georgian coughed twice. General Custis rocked on his heels, studying Shell. It was Custis who spoke next.

"Can you get to Chicamauga, Captain Morgan?"

"Possibly. It's practically home to me. With a small group of men."

"In civilian clothes?" Custis had asked.

"Sir," the tall captain had replied, "I took an oath that I wouldn't take off the gray until the war was over."

"It is over, damnit!" Fainer shouted.

"And lost, Morgan," General Custis said flatly. "Without vast, immediately assistance. *That* is what I'm asking you to win for us."

Shelter Morgan stood there, blue-gray eyes sweeping over the gathered officers. Some of them he did not like personally—like the aristocratic Leland Mason—yet that did not enter into his thoughts now.

What they asked was nearly impossible. And if caught in civilian clothes he would be summarily shot, as he well knew. Yet they had asked him because he knew that region well; because they trusted him to return with the gold if anyone could. He nodded his head slowly.

"I'll do it. If I can, sir, I will do it. Let me pick my own men and set my own route."

"Of course," Colonel Fainer said, rising, a smile painted on his broad mouth. He stuck out his hand and Shell took it. "You'll make it, son, if anyone can."

And they did—almost.

With four handpicked men Shelter had ridden the ridges and creekbottoms to Lookout. A Union sharpshooter had taken Keane, the Kentuckian out of his saddle as they crested a ridge, and Jeb Thornton was carrying lead, but

11

remarkably had made it, under Sherman's nose, riding under cover of darkness, hiding in the deepest thickets in the daylight hours. They had made it.

Almost.

Coming into the clearing not far from the Conasauga they were met by what was left of General Curtis' army. Fainer was there, Mason, Major Twyner, and the general himself—fifteen others, half of them enlisted men. And they all carried guns, guns which were levelled on Morgan. Every man-jack of them was dressed in civilian clothes.

"What is this?" Morgan had asked.

"It's what you think," Fainer had answered, nearly apologetically, Shell thought. He had followed Fainer through some hard fighting; he had thought they were close. Now they were only as close as a bullet.

Who shot first, Shell was never certain, but the clearing exploded with gunpowder, rearing horses, and the shrieks of pain. Jeb Thornton had gone down first, shot through the chest, trampled by his pony. Welton Williams, firing coolly, giving not an inch had been torn to ribbons. Dinkum had lasted until nightfall, dying with his head sumberged in the cold, bloody Conasauga—three good men dead because of Shell, dead through betrayal, greed.

Only Shell had survived. And he was clapped into a Union prison for nearly two years while the officers and men of the battalion, fat with gold, spread out across the country, living new lives as if their sins had been forgotten.

Perhaps they had been—but Shelter had not forgotten.

Still at night he heard the roar of guns, saw the familiar faces of the betrayers. The dead forms of Thornton, Williams and Dinkum.

Briefly he thought of the winter in the Colorado mountains, of Captain Leland Mason, then Shell's eyes snapped open. Somehow he had fallen off to sleep. Linda, propped up on one elbow, lay beside him.

"Were you dreaming about it again?" she asked. "Your face . . . it's a terrible thing you carry with you, Shelter. Your face was twisted with it. Then suddenly, just before you woke up, you smiled."

"I was thinking of Leland Mason," Shell replied. He ran a finger down Linda's soft shoulder, watching her mouth.

"You hated him!" she said with surprise. "You shot him to death."

"Yes," Shell replied grimly.

Linda was silent, not comprehending. "*That* could make you smile?" She shook her head. "I was hoping you were thinking of me," she added coyly.

"No," Shell answered soberly. "But I am now."

She laughed and buried her head against his chest, her long blond hair tumbling over his chest.

"Are you sure you were asleep?" Linda asked.

"I was. Asleep, having a nightmare."

13

"Only a part of you was sleeping," Linda said into his ear. Her hand ran down across his hard muscled abdomen, finding his cock still swollen, ready.

"Him? He don't sleep much," Shell said wryly.

"I can make you forget your nightmare again—for a little while," Linda promised him.

"Can you?"

Shell drew her near; sweeping the hair from her mouth he kissed it deeply, his hand finding her nipples which were taut, eager.

"Yes," Linda breathed.

Shell lay on his back, his hands behind his head. Linda threw back the sheets and on hands and knees she swept his body with kisses: thighs, ankles, chest and abdomen—searching, sucking kisses which raised Shell's erection even farther. Linda buried her head between his legs and lay still a long moment, her hands wrapped around his thighs, loving the man-smell about him, the hard rippling muscles beneath his skin.

She sat up suddenly and turned her back to Shell, throwing a knee across him as she settled on his erection, spreading herself with her fingers as she slid slowly up and down.

Shell studied her, enjoying the sight of her slim, naked back, her full, blemishless buttocks, the cascading blond hair as much as the sensation between his legs.

Still Linda slid along his length, the concentration evident in the taut muscles across her back, the quivering which had begun beneath the white skin of her hips.

Shell ran his hands down her spine, from neck to buttocks, and she responded as a cat might, with a rippling of the muscles, a flexing of her spine.

"Shell . . ."

Her excitement was obvious. Shell could feel the warmth of her body across his abdomen and Linda leaned suddenly forward, lifting his cock, and as Shell watched she held it poised, settling slowly onto it.

Linda's head was bent far forward, her hair spread out across Shell's thighs. She still held his erection, and looking back between her legs she could see not only the rigid, red tipped cock slowly entering her, but the face of the blue eyed man who owned it.

She leaned far forward, watching as if she were another person as she slipped the tip of his erection into her moist sanctuary, manipulating it so that it stroked her taut clitoris then her cervix, feeling her inner walls become a sheath of nerve endings all crying for one resolution.

She sank slowly onto him, still watching, her pulse racing as she took him to the hilt. Then she sat upright, unsteadily and began swaying back and forth. Linda reached back with her hands and Shell took them as she slowly lifted herself and then settled back on him.

Shell arched his back, lifting her and she began a swaying, rolling motion, clenching his hand as she moved to a secret rhythm.

She was hot, slick within and Shell responded to her with another thrust. Linda moaned, tore at her own hair and leaned forward, bracing herself against Shell's thighs with her hands.

Slowly then she rocked forward, back so that Shell could see himself entering her. He touched her hips, her inner lips and Linda shuddered, driving against him, wanting to feel him to her depths.

"Now . . ." she moaned and her head moved from side to side in a primitive response. "Now!" she shrieked out loud, but Shell held himself back, wanting her to reach her hard climax.

She breathed raggedly, clenching his thighs as if she would tear them apart and her hips rose and fell.

"God!" she muttered and she trembled, going limp, her warm juices trickling down her thigh as Shell began moving slowly, methodically, bringing her up again to a second climax, his own needs pushing him on.

Roughly he grabbed her hips now and thrust deeply against her and Linda caved in as he reached a driving, rolling climax. She sat utterly still, her hair draped across his legs. Then she gave another tiny shudder, and Shell could feel the muscles within her rippling, contracting.

"Shell . . ." She turned around, clumsily, unsteadily as if the blood had gone out of her. Her eyes unfocused, an earthy smile parted her lips.

Without losing him she managed to turn then lay atop of him, listening to the pounding of his heart as she stroked his chest, running her fingers through the blond hair there.

They were silent, still for a long moment, then she turned her head toward the window.

"What is it?" he asked her.

"It must rain again. It must," she breathed into his ear.

But late morning brought a clearing in the weather. The high, jumbled clouds spawned a fantastic golden fan where the sun pierced them. At nightfall a light wind arose, pushing the storm southward and the stars like lost children reappeared in the black, utterly clear skies over Colorado.

It would be in the morning then—Shell made the decision with what amounted to relief. It was time to be tracking, and now he could concentrate entirely on it, knowing he would not be delayed further.

Linda had left a note pinned to her pillow and he picked it up with a brief smile. He turned it over in his hands, started to open it and then set it down on the bureau. There was no time for long goodbyes or long remembrances.

If it was ever all over . . .

Shell shook his head, glancing as his own lean face in the mirror. A man has so many chances. He had already used up plenty of them. To hope that he might last all the way through this . . . He picked up his razor and stropped it on his boot.

Mason had been tough—Wakefield too. It was a wonder they hadn't put Shelter down for good. He touched his shoulder. It was still sore, a reminder.

Shell finished his dry shave and dampened his hair, frowning at his mirror image. A lanky, flat jawed man with deep blue-gray eyes, carrying most of his weight in his chest and shoulders stared back from the clouded mirror.

"We've a long ways to go," Shell told the man in the mirror.

There were too many ways a man could get it. A shot from a darkened alley, a fire where he slept, an unseen sharpshooter on some lonesome ridge . . . a man has to be a fool sometimes.

Shell walked down through the empty hotel lobby where a lantern burned low behind the deserted counter, and out onto the boardwalk.

The night was cold, still. Few folks were on the street. It was late for the townfolks and early for the drinkers. He strode the long plankwalk, enjoying the cold air in his lungs. The distant, broken notes of a piano reached his ears.

Across the street and up, the Fountainebleau where Linda used to sing sat dark, boarded up. That had been Leland Mason's place. It gave Shell a sense of righteousness to see it dark, empty.

Yet there was a residual bitterness as well.

He shrugged it off and walked into the Butter & Eggs Restaurant where supper was being served by a heavy woman in a starched apron to some miners at a long plank table, and to a weary, pouch-eyed drummer who sat at the counter.

Shell stood in the doorway, looking around the room. The few who knew him ignored him. Then

18

he spotted Turpin at a corner table and he lifted a hand.

The prospector had his boots off. On the table before him was a stack of empty platters, a coffee pot, and on his bearded face a contented smile.

"Sit down, Morgan," Turpin invited.

"What's good enough to eat, Abe?" Shell asked, hooking a chair with his boot, pulling it out as he tossed his hat on the empty table beside them.

"Everything," Abe Turpin said with a satis-fied smile. "I've tried some of each, and it's all fittin'."

"Can't believe you got all that in you," Shell said, looking at the empty platters where pork chop bones rested in gravy, bare beef rib bones beside them. The plate before Turpin had some well-gnawed pig knuckles. The prospector grin-ned toothlessly, scratching his sparse, graying beard and burped.

"I did—pardon the excess there—and enjoyed every bite. I spent a year and a half in the desert, Shelter. Nothing but damned sourdough and beans, rabbit and whatever else I could catch up. Ate a hooty owl once . . . this is heaven to me. Close as I want to get . . . close as they'll let me," he added on reflection.

The waitress, smelling faintly of powder and perspiration stood over them, hands on hips. She surveyed Shelter Morgan coolly.

"Don't tell me you want the same," she said warily.

"No." Shell laughed. "Steak, eggs and taters with coffee."

"*You're* a gentleman," she sighed, sparing a scathing glance for Abe Turpin.

She collected an armful of platters, leaving the coffee pot at Abe's insistence. "Mebbe you got an apple pie!" he called after her.

"Think she does?" Turpin asked Shell. Wistfully he said. "Haven't had a slab of apple pie since . . . '62, I believe, . . . I take it you're ridin' soon."

"I am," Shelter answered, pouring coffee from Abe's pot into his own cup. It was hot, bitter.

"I figured. Soon as I seen those skies clearing, I thought of you. You can't be talked out of it?"

"No. I can't be."

"Didn't figure so." Turpin shook his head and chuckled.

"I know a hard-headed bull buffalo when I run across one." He grinned at Shell. "No offense intended."

"None taken. I've been labeled worse than that."

"So have I," Turpin agreed, "and often enough that bein' called a buffalo would be a compliment to me. But you say you're going after Plum, come what may."

"I am. If he's the same man, and from your description, I'm almost certain of it."

The waitress had returned and Shell dropped his elbows off the table long enough for her to slap down a platter with a two-inch thick steak on it, and another with three eggs and fried potatoes.

"You two must work awful hard," the waitress said, wiping back a strand of hair. "There's miners couldn't eat half that."

"I work it off," Shell said, cutting at his meat.

"I'll bet you do," the waitress said. She turned to go, and Turpin hollered after her.

"Don't forget that pie!" He filled his coffee cup again and leaned forward, watching Shell chew his meat.

"Now this man Plum," Abe began, "I'm not right sure when he come into the Painted Gorge area. But I'd reckon late in '66. I was up in the Dragoons, panning a little dust and when I come back down, damned if I didn't run into fencing, branded cows and a sure enough house thrown up along Carizo—adobe house it was."

The waitress was back with a deep dish apple pie. Abe nodded and began cutting into it.

"I rode on up to his house—not having seen a man with a white face in near twenty months. Damned if he didn't cuss me for a desert coyote and order me off."

Shell frowned. That was unusual, defensive. Generally speaking westerners welcomed company, the times between visitors being extended, the ranches far apart. A cowboy was welcome to bed down and eat his fill—between jobs many a cowhand survived by riding the grubline, accepting meals for odd jobs.

Most ranch houses were left unlocked, and a wandering hand whether in Arizona or Montana was liable to find a note such as: "Help yourself to bacon and flour. Feed the chickens if you

21

please," or some such tacked onto the door.

"Unfriendly as hell," Shell commented, breaking the yolk of an egg, dipping his potatoes in it.

"Of course folks are right shy just now—got a Chiricahua renegade named Thumb lifting folks' hair and raising bloody hell in that territory just now ... it's a bad time to ride south." Abe glanced at Shell, but the remark seemed to have no effect on the tall, blond-headed man.

"But Plum saw you face to face—he didn't take you for an Apache."

"No. Course I could have been taken for anything after the dry spell I'd had. He didn't take me for no Chireecahua, Morgan. Thing was—what did he take me for? The man don't want no visitors, I'll tell you that. Mebbe it's *you* he's expectin'."

"I hope not. But he should be." Shell sipped at his steaming coffee and studied what he had learned thoughtfully. Plum had every right to be cautious. A killer, with a spread built on his take of the stolen gold. "He keep many hands around?" Shell wanted to know.

"Well, not so many," Abe Turpin answered around the last mouthful of pie, "but them I did see, Morgan—they were carryin' a plenty of firepower. Guns pokin' out every which a way." He paused then added, "It'll be a hard ride. I like you, son ... you ought to look to your health. What Virgil Plum done is a horrible thing, but you're a young man with a lot of life ahead of you. I'd hate to see you lose what's due you—them years."

"So would I," Shell replied. "But it's mine to do."

Abe Turpin nodded. He could understand it. A man can't back away from himself, from his obligations.

"I'll do what I can to lay out the territory for you." Turpin said. "But if you ain't been across that desert, you won't know until you're up against it what I'm talkin' about. It's a dreadful, fierce land, Morgan, with everything that lives covered with spines or leather hide—a man has to get that way too. You'll walk salt playas so wide you'll think you'll never see water again, dunes a man and his horse can disappear into, and always the rattlers and the scorpions. Let alone the Chiricahua. But I'll he'p you if I can. If you're determined that the desert is where you want to leave your bones."

2.

The Butterfield stage station was at the tag end of Colorado Boulevard. It was locked up when Shell arrived at six-thirty in the morning, so he tossed his saddle onto the boardwalk, leaned the Winchester against the wall and waited.

In a moment a harried, spectacled man appeared, fishing a key from his vest pocket. He glanced at Shell, scarcely nodded, and unlocked the door.

"Mornin'," Shell responded. He scraped the red mud from his boots and followed the station clerk inside.

"Thought that Fort Union stage would be harnessed up and ready to roll by now," Shell commented idly. He fingered the pen at the counter as the clerk rushed around, unlocking a wire-enclosed shipping dock, pulling out a manifest of some kind which he slapped on the counter.

"Fort Union stage will be delayed," the clerk said.

"How long?"

The clerk looked up, his eyes magnified behind those thick bifocals. He shook his head.

"Can't say. Maybe an hour . . ." then he looked again at Shell, hard. "Isn't your name Morgan?"

"It is."

"Heard about you. You were a deputy marshal, weren't you?"

"Not exactly. I worked with Marshal Buckaloo for a few days, that's all."

"So I heard," the little man said thoughtfully. "I heard how you worked. It'll be at least an hour," he said, suddenly shifting tracks.

"All right. I'll wait."

Shell settled onto the bench which ran nearly the length of the front wall, watching the clerk race here and there, shouting something out the alley door. He tipped his hat forward, crossed his arms and rested.

The sound of the clerk talking to someone else brought Shell's eyes open. A burly white man

25

with slicked down hair and a big cigar was looking closely at Shell.

"You Morgan?" the big man asked.

"That's me," Shell allowed. The big man beckoned to him and he crossed the room to the counter where the big man surveyed him closely.

"Going through to Fort Union?"

"If things ever get rollin'."

"We've had some trouble down the line. Lost a team and a driver." The man hesitated and added, "My name's Moffitt—I'm the Butterfield agent here. You know what the fare is through to Union, Morgan?"

"Sixty-eight dollars, the man told me."

"How'd you like to ride free?" Moffitt asked abruptly. Shell frowned and he hastily added, "Plus twenty to boot."

"What's the deal?" Shell asked.

"We're short of people, and we're carrying a load," Moffitt said, and by the way he said it, Shell figured the "load" was valuable. Maybe a gold shipment from the mines.

"What do you need?"

"Cummins here tells me you're a fighting man. I'd like you to ride shotgun for us, Morgan. Just through to Fort Union—you're riding anyway, it'll make you a few bucks."

"You're expecting trouble," Shell said and Moffitt swallowed and nodded.

"To be truthful, yes."

Shell was thoughtful for a moment, then he said, "I'll take the twenty in gold."

"You'll do it?"

"I will—truth is, if there's trouble coming I'd rather be up on the box where I can see it coming."

It was another half an hour before the stage drew up before the Butterfield office, the driver a whip-lean red-mustached man tying the reins around the brake handle before he clambered down, appraising Shell.

"You Morgan?"

"I am,"

"Climb up. We're runnin' empty as far as Pueblo, and Moffit's havin' a fit about the schedule." The driver spat out a stream of tobacco, coloring the boardwalk. "Truth to tell, we ain't been on time since I've been makin' the Southern run. Five hours is the nearest I've managed—and that time I had a bunch of Arapahoes behind me, enouraging it."

Shell climbed up, settling in the box. Moffitt and the driver reappeared carrying a heavy, iron-banded box which they placed in the boot as the clerk, looking unsure of himself, held an express gun, glancing up and down Colorado Boulevard.

"That's it?" Shell asked as the driver climbed back up.

"That's it." He spat tobacco juice against the haunch of the bay gelding below him, gathered up the ribbons and slapped the brake free.

"Heyawh!" He slapped the reins against the flanks of the wheel horse and the team bolted forward, the coach sliding through the red ooze of the road, splashing up a wake of mud as the team ran flat out the length of Colorado

Boulevard, around the north bend and onto the southbound road toward Pueblo, a hundred and fifty miles away.

Shell was holding to his hat with one hand, to the rail with the other as the coach rolled onto the long flat valley. The driver slowed the team down to an easy pace and with a smile he told Shell:

"I always run 'em out of town—makes Moffitt think I'm accomplishin' somethin'." He turned his head and cautiously spat some tobacco juice. "My name's Dendy," he told Shell. "True name's George, but with a handle like mine folks change it around, so I'm Jim Dandy to most."

"Moffitt seemed to be expecting trouble," Shell commented.

"Naw." Dendy wagged his head. "There's been some down south—stick-ups, and east with the Arapaho. Damned fool name of Plunkett stirred that up."

"The Arapaho trouble?"

"Yeah. They come up on Plunkett outside of Julesburg. Wanted one of Plunkett's horses—probably fixin' to eat it, but Plunk—he wanted to make a fight of it. Upshot was we lost a team and got a coach burned. Shotgun rider was scared off into the hills." Dendy spat again, wiping his mouth with the sleeve of his faded red shirt.

"Anything like that ever happen to you?"

"Son," Dendy said, "I've had every burden you can imagine laid on me. I've been shot at, flooded out ... attacked once by an old lady wielding a parasol. Seems I made her crumple her favorite hat . . . I had it happen.

"Utes it was, some years back, they were friendly enough, but you never know. I cut an animal out of the harness and laid a whip on the other three gettin' into Leadville. Caught hell for it, too."

Dendy had a hundred stories and Shell listened politely. But the stories rushed by like the wind. Shell's eyes were on the magnificent sweep of snow-laced mountains, the endless ranks of virgin timber; his mind was on other people, other times.

They nooned at the Camden stage stop, eating a meal of sourdough, beans and venison while the dour-faced Camden changed horses.

"Watch your butt, Dendy," Camden said as he handed the reins up. "Somebody has made up their mind that Butterfield's easy pickin's. Got the word out of Pueblo this morning—lost another shipment, driver killed."

"Who was he?"

"Corbett," the man replied.

"Frank Corbett never had a lick of sense anyway," Dendy said sourly.

"That's the trouble with you," Camden told him, "you can't take nothin serious. *You*, Shotgun, you keep your eyes open. These folks ain't fools. They know the Leadville run will be carryin' Army gold."

"Who says I got gold?" Jim Dandy asked, biting off a chaw of tobacco. "Nothin' but corset stays and molasses back there."

Camden wiped his jaw, studying the red-mustached driver, then Shell once again. "*You* watch out for him." Camden said. "Damn fool ain't got the brains to watch hisself."

Shell promised that he would, with a sidelong grin at Dendy who spat, snapped the reins and set off again, rolling across the plank bridge, beneath the twin oaks which shaded the road.

Dendy was cool, no doubt he had made too many of these runs to get gun-shy. If he was that sort they would have run him off years ago. Still Shell could read the apprehension beneath the leathery hide and he rode loose as well, eyes scouring the broken timberland, the brushy flatlands to the east.

The afternoon was cool, the land empty as they trailed dust through Gunnison Canyon, high red bluffs rising above them. The water rushed through the streambed beside the road where cottonwoods, still bare with winter interwove ghostly, mottled branches.

The long grade topped out on a bald knob where the wind rushed over them, rocking the stage as the horses blew. Shell climbed down and shook his head, not liking what he saw.

Below them, spread out across what seemed half the world was a vast red basin dusted with scant greasewood and sage, here and there a lone pine.

The basin was nearly two thousand feet below where they rested, and the trail down was a series of narrow switchbacks winding through the rocky passes barren of growth.

"A likely stretch of road, ain't it?" Dendy said.

"Likely for anyone who wanted to stop us," Shell replied. There was no way to outrun anyone on that steep, winding grade, no way to avoid trouble if it came. They could only hope that luck was with them, that the gang which had been plaguing Butterfield was not as smart as Camden thought.

"If they know we got gold," Dendy said as if reading Shell's thoughts, "they'd likely try to take us on the grade. Once into the basin, it's a dead flat run to Pueblo."

Shell climbed back into the box, tugging his hat low against the glare of the sun. The Winchester which had rested beside his leg he now carried across his lap.

Dendy moved the coach out, easing down the long, narrow grade, riding the brake and reins. Shell rode silently. The coach jolted over rocks washed down by the recent heavy rains. In the canyons it was cool, dark, a wind whistling down the passes. There was that followed by the brilliant sunlight and a breathtaking view of the deep basin below where a single strand of road lined southward.

Dendy whistled and cussed his horses, guiding them with sure, practiced hands. Here and there the trail was washed out, and below a drop of a thousand feet or more, and above white, stone covered bluffs ready to slide free at any whim of gravity.

They took more than two hours to cover the next three miles. Twice Shell had to climb from the box to roll aside boulders, each time wondering if this was it—if those rocks had been rolled purposely.

There were deep, water cut clefts in those hills which could have hidden a hundred men and their horses and sudden, treacherous hairpin turns where the wagon wheels hung on the very lip of the trail, showering rocks down toward the valley floor.

As they dropped the temperature had risen and now, five hundred feet or so above the empty basin, a warm wind drafted across the gorges. The horses were sweat-caked, and Dendy's arms were wooden.

The road circled a last rocky knob and then rolled out onto the basin floor, straightening out on the level ground. Dendy turned to Shell.

"I guess they . . ."

It was then that the guns opened up. The wheel horse went to his hind legs, pawing at the air and Dendy's mouth filled with blood, the reins falling from his hands as the sharp volley of shots echoed up the canyons.

Shell looked up, saw the gleam of sun on steel and fired off-handedly. He grabbed for Dendy but the man sagged forward, going to the floor of the box, the reins falling beneath the stampeding team.

Shell hesitated a split second longer, then clutching his Winchester he leaped free of the stage, landing with a bone crunching thud, the dust from the coach billowing over him as he rolled aside, a bullet tearing up the earth beside him.

Shell staggered to his feet, Winchester at hip level. He saw a man in a blue shirt pop out from behind a rock, and he fired, hearing the angry whine of a ricochet as the man yelled, leaping behind a massive white boulder.

Another shot slammed into the earth near Shell and he knew it was move or die, the odds being what they were. With a shudder he looked down the hundred feet of rocky canyon below him and threw himself off, rolling through flesh tearing manzanita and scrub oak, scrambling wildly downslope until his foot slipped and he went down, jolting the breath from his body against a nearly square, yellowish boulder just as an angry bullet whipped through the air near his head.

It might have been that which saved him. Perhaps the marksman had figured that his bullet had taken Shell, perhaps they simply felt no need to pursue the shotgun rider into the brush clotted ravine where they themselves would offer open targets.

Whichever way it was, Shell was down, his head reeling, breath ragged in his chest, Winchester clenched firmly. It was silent above him, the dust drifting slowly away. Sweat trickled down Shell's forehead, burning his eyes. His side was badly bruised, perhaps a rib had been cracked. He shifted slightly, and winced with the pain.

It was already coming dark, the film of clouds above the distant high Rockies going purple as long shadows crept out of the canyons, claiming the earth.

Shell took a chance and shifted positions, scrambling to a deeper clump of brush where he sat, Winchester propped up, searching the trail above him, the rocky knoll where the holdup men had been.

He figured now to wait until dark, using the night to cover him. Then he would move. Move where?

He scanned the canyon above and then below him where it spilled out onto the basin. There was no sign of movement, no sound. They could then, still be above, watching.

Shelter thought he had nicked one of them, but even of that he could not be sure. And Dendy? He had been hit bad. Yet possibly he was alive up there on the trail—if the coach was still there.

He had no knowledge of the landfall around here, except for the glimpse he had gotten from above. Was there another trail branching off the main road, or would the holdup men have to ride back up the grade?

Or down—that made more sense. That way they would be riding away from Leadville and any pursuit. Shell leaned his head back against the still warm rock at his back. Lifting his shirt he examined his side by the twilight. A huge, splotched bruise covered his ribs on the left side. A nasty yellow and purple thing, still he did not feel a sharp pain as he fingered his side, searching gingerly for any sign of a broken rib.

He waited then, eyes alert, sweat cooling on his body as night settled across the empty, alien land. He would have to go back up, he decided.

A horse—that was the first thing. It was doubtful the bandits would have made off with the horses, although not impossible. But Shell needed a horse, and he did not kid himself about how much he needed one. The land below was wide, waterless perhaps. And he a stranger to it.

Without a horse a man would die. Shelter Morgan had no intention of dying—there was too much left undone.

The wind was cold now, off the distant peaks. The night crystalline, starlit. No moon illuminated the rocky hillside, but by starlight Shell was able to pick his way slowly up toward the road, surprised at how far he had fallen and rolled.

It took a good half hour to climb to the trail, and by that time Shell was covered with sweat, chilled by the blasts of wind down the long slopes. Glancing up the road, then toward the knoll, Shell walked on in the direction the stagecoach had taken.

There was no sign of fire, no smell of woodsmoke—he had expected none. The outlaws had probably ridden far and fast.

By the faint silver light Shell could make out the tracks of the coach clearly as he walked cautiously around the knob, eyes flickering to the dark hillside. The sweat was cool on his chest, his side throbbing, mouth dry as he moved forward.

A deep shadow from the knob itself lay across the road and as Shell cleared it he stopped abruptly. The wagon tracks were gone!

Frowning he retraced his steps, searching the road closely. Nothing.

They were there, then simply gone.

Something caught his eye. Beside the road, on a low sumac limb . . . a hat. He recognized it for Dendy's and picked it up. It was only then that he saw it—a fork trail obviously seldom-used, wound down on that side of the trail, and there were fresh wagon tracks cut into the earth.

A movement, a shadow caught Shell's attention suddenly and he spun, levering a shell into the Winchester. It was a man and Shelter slowly lowered the rifle.

Dendy lay concealed in the brush, his clothing torn, eyes white in the starlight. Yet his hand moved and Shell clawed through the brushy ravine toward the driver. He was alive.

Broken and beat up, but alive. He opened his mouth and gripped Shell's shirt front.

"I got you," Shell said softly. "We'll make it out."

"Not likely . . ." Dendy said, a blood-choked laugh rattling in his throat.

"*You* going to be the pessimist suddenly!" Shell said with a smile. Dendy smiled back, weakly. Shelter put his Winchester in the crotch of a low growing manzanita and gathered some brush to make a pillow for the driver. When he was done, folding his shirt over the boughs for some added comfort, he gently shifted Dendy, bringing a gasp of pain from the driver's lips.

"Where'd they get you, Dendy?"

The driver touched his chest and Shell carefully spread Dendy's shirt, lifting the cloth from the scab. It was a bad one; even by the faint light, Shell could see there was little he could do. He bandaged it with the tail torn from his shirt, Dendy quietly submitting to the lifting and prodding.

There was perspiration glossing Dendy's face although the night was chill by the time Shell was done. "Now what, nurse?" he asked with a wavering smile.

"I'm going to carry you out of here," Shell said.

"Not likely. It's forty miles to Pueblo. Twenty to Twin Oaks—that's the nearest settlement."

"And the next stage through?" Shell asked.

"Three days," Dendy told him. "Of course they may start out a posse from Pueblo if we don't show by tomorrow afternoon—two days it would take them. Doesn't matter," Dendy said, closing his eyes. "I couldn't make it on horseback anyway, even sayin' somebody from Pueblo comes."

Shell sat back on his heels, mouth set. Those were the options then—wait or try to carry Dendy out when both of them knew they couldn't make a trek like that.

Dendy's head tossed from side to side restlessly. Shell had not even water to give the man, and he dared not start a fire.

"You . . ." Dendy lifted his head with great effort. "You walk on out, Morgan."

"Like Hell," Shelter answered softly.

He felt helpless, and he hated that feeling more

than any other. As long as a man could plan, fight, move, he could feel he was accomplishing even if in reality he was doing little. But to sit and wait, seeing no answer was a frustrating thing.

"This old road," Shell asked, "where does it go?"

"South Fork? Nowhere. Used to be a stage station there five years back, but the Indians burned it. There's no help in that direction." Dendy straightened up slightly. "But that's not what you're thinkin', is it?"

"No, it isn't." Shell was approaching the problem from a different direction and Dendy had guessed it.

"You're crazy," the driver said, sagging back.

"Am I? They went that way, didn't they? They've got everything we need—horses, the stage."

"You'll just get your ownself killed as well. Walk out, Morgan—I can't blame you."

"I'd blame myself," Shelter said. It was a hair-raising notion, tracking after those outlaws. Yet otherwise Dendy would surely die. It there was even a chance they'd abandoned the coach, why not have a look-see?

"They see you, they'll kill you."

"I reckon. I'll have to prevent that. I've walked a few night patrols in my time. Some said I was a regular Indian at it."

"They've got guns."

"If I recall, the Yankees used to carry 'em too. We got away with some of the damndest tricks

38

at night from time to time . . ."

"But you know what happens when you don't get away with it." Dendy waved a hand and added. "Never thought I'd meet another man as stubborn as me."

Shell smiled in the darkness. But it wasn't sheer stubbornness which prodded him, nor any special courage. It was only the knowledge that something needed to be done if Dendy was to live.

There might not be a chance in Hades of catching up with the outlaws, of even finding them, let alone recapturing the stage . . . but then again there just might be that chance. He had to take it.

Shelter rose, quietly taking up his Winchester and Dendy's hat which he meant to impale on a twig near the road so that a passer-by might find the driver. There was always the faint chance that someone might be on that desolate stretch of road.

Dendy's eyes opened halfway.

"Goin' to play Injun, are you?"

"I am," Shell replied.

"Play it good," Dendy said, his eyes fluttering closed as Shell turned away, inhaling deeply the cold mountain air, his eyes searching the long empty hillsides where nothing was to be seen. The starlight barely illuminated the overgrown South Fork trail winding off through the chaparral and Shell stepped off down it, rifle easy in the crook of his arm, the cold night surrounding him.

The tracks were easy enough to follow, even

with this light. The stagecoach had broken the new growth of brush down and the broken twigs showed white against the blackness of the hillsides.

He walked for a good hour, only once losing the trail across a stretch of bare rock. They still had the coach with them. Did that mean anything?

It might have been that the stage was the easiest way to carry a heavy chest of gold—it would have broken down a saddle horse. Yet they could have broken the strongbox open and divided it up . . . maybe someone didn't want to divide it up. Not equally.

It was funny how greedy folks could get around gold. Especially those who came by their gold by stealing it. Oftentimes they would work together only long enough to accomplish their crime, each of them all along having ideas on how to increase his share . . .

Shell stopped stone dead. There was something in the air. He crept slowly toward the next hillrise, getting off the trail as far as he dared, figuring any guard would be watching the trail and not the surrounding hills.

It came again in the air—the faint scent of woodsmoke and Shell searched the tiny teacup valley below him for the tell-tale glow of a fire. There was none. If there was a fire in that valley, it was under cover, in a stand of trees or perhaps a cave. Maybe, he conjectured, the fire had been extinguished, leaving only the lingering smell in the night air. It could be that they had wanted a fire only long enough to cook, to split the take.

By the position of the Big Dipper's handle against the black sky, Shell guess it was nearly four in the morning. There had been a full moon rising toward dawn this week. That meant he had two hours more or less to find the camp, recover the stage if possible, and get back to Dendy.

Then what? They would surely follow . . . Shell got to his feet and moved on. That bridge would have to be crossed later.

Silently he circled to the west, dropping down into the valley through a broken stand of oak trees. The starlight cast weird, wavering shadows across the frosted grass of the valley. A low winging owl circled low, spotted Shell and climbed away, cutting a ghostly silhouette.

The fire scent was gone, had been for some time and still Shell could see nothing, nor hear a sound—he had hoped a restless horse might nicker or shift his feet—such sounds would carry far in the night.

He was nearly into their camp before he saw it.

There were two men sleeping on the ground under an oak, another near the stagecoach. Five horses stood tied to a line across the clearing, and the stage horses were still hitched!

Unhitching the team would have meant only extra work to these men, and from their line of work, Shell knew they were not concerned with anything like that.

His eyes darted around the clearing, searching.

Five saddle horses they had, but there were only three men sleeping. A guard at the road on either side? Likely.

And since those men had not taken their horses, it was likely they were close in.

Was the gold on the stage? *That* was not likely, and Shell couldn't let that bother him just now anyway. Let Butterfield come after that gold if they wanted it. Shell wanted only the coach, although as he looked over the camp, the short, rugged road back toward where Dendy lay, it seemed less than possible.

Sucking in a small breath, Shell moved slowly around the camp perimeter, freezing as a twig snapped underfoot. He cursed the misstep silently and watched. One man rolled over in his soogan then settled again to sleep.

Stars spattered the velvet sky overhead. Deep shadows blotted out the mountains. It was cold —Shell's breath steamed out in tiny wisps as he moved on cat feet toward the stage.

Still as it was, one mistake could fill the clearing with fire and smoke, the flashing of guns, and Shell knew it well.

He had reached the horses. A white faced bay nudged him with its nose, shifting its feet, and Shell patted its neck quieting it as he untied the tethering line. The horses were free now, but they did not know it. They stood still out of habit and Shell slid between them, eyes going again and again to the camp.

The outlaw sleeping under the coach seemed to be having a peaceful dream, and it seemed a shame to take that away from him. Shell lifted the butt of his Winchester and swung out with it. The man never even stirred; there was only the dent in his hat to show he was sleeping a bit more deeply.

Shell crept along the side of the coach, taking a quick peek inside to make sure no one was sleeping inside. He climbed into the box, unwrapping the reins. The brake squeaked a protest as he released it, and Shell turned his head sharply. Still they had not awakened, and it seemed a shame to do it now.

But there was only one way to turn that coach around—by circling it right through their camp.

Shell flicked the reins gently and tugged the wheel horse to the right. Lazily he moved out, the wheels squeaking faintly, the trace chains clinking. A man sat up in his bed, grabbed for his gun and Shell yelled out whipping the horse to a full run.

Shell's pistol was out as well, and he fired a shot over the heads of the saddle horses. They broke free, running into the darkness, eyes wild, frightened as Shell wheeled the stage through the outlaw camp.

A shot slammed against the stagecoach box, and a man yelled as the stage rolled through the dead fire and over an outlaw's bed, the man scrambling madly to escape the pounding hoofs, the heavy wheels of the coach.

The night was filled with gunfire. Shell ducked low and slapped the reins, urging the horses on up the dark, brush clotted trail, barely visible in the night.

A last shot sang overhead as it missed, wide high, and Shell glanced back toward the outlaw camp, seeing a shadowy figure in the road, hands on hips.

How long would it take them to round up their horses? There was no way of telling. But in the darkness, in that terrain, maybe enough.

Yet even if that held true, he was not out of this yet—not by a damned sight.

There was a sentry somewhere up ahead. A sentry who had picked his spot and would be alert to trouble after the shooting. Shell slowed the ponies and searched the series of low hills above the old coach trail.

Yet it was unlikely he would see anything until the shooting started.

The pale moon was breaking the horizon to the east, glossing the basin below with an eerie glow. Shell eased the horses upward, saving them for a run. He had no idea if anyone was following yet, though they soon would be, had no idea when the shooting would begin . . . only that it would.

The stage crept up the slow, broken road as the moon rose higher, bringing a weird false dawn to the low hills. There was a last sharp crest to be made, then the road angled down sharply, running in a nearly straight path toward the main road where Dendy lay.

Maybe, Shell thought hopefully, I was wrong. Maybe these outlaws were a sloppy bunch, posting no sentries, feeling secure in their strength, the remoteness of the area.

No sooner had that thought cleared his mind

than the rifle on the hillrise sang out and the wheel horse reared up in panic.

Shell saw the flash of flame high on the dark hill and he fired just to let the man know he had teeth, although nothing was visible. Again the rifle on the hill fired, and long echo rumbling down the canyon and Shell ducked low into the box of the stage, whipping the horses with the reins, trusting to their instincts.

He lifted his head slightly and another shot slammed into the driver's box, showering him with splinters, but the horses were running. Running hard, the stage careening around a turn in the trail, jolting over a large rock.

But by now they were out of range, out of sight and Shell could straighten up, slowing the horses who had not wandered from the trail, perhaps following their own scent back toward the main road.

The moon rose slowly. A white, waning full moon. Yet now it was an ally, a friendly sight as it lighted the trail, showing the dangerous washes and boulders strewn across the little used road.

It was another half hour before Shell spotted the rocky knob which marked the fork in the road and now he moved the horses faster, worrying about Dendy.

The man had been seriously wounded. Had he even lasted the night? Assuming he had, could he survive the jolting ride into Pueblo? The outlaws were back there somewhere; but perhaps they would give it up . . . that was a faint hope, but Shell clung to it.

The stage climbed up onto the main road and Shell halted the horses. They stood there, blowing hard as Shell leaped from the coach, going to where he had left Dendy.

He lay there still, unmoving.

"Dendy!" Shelter crouched beside him, gently shaking his shoulder. Dead? No, his eyes flickered open. Listless, colorless eyes they focused finally on Shelter Morgan.

"How'd the Injunin' go?"

"I got the coach. I got to get you inside. They might be a-comin'."

"I'd as soon lay here and die," Dendy whispered.

"You're not gettin' that wish. Come on! This is no time to give up."

"Ain't it? It sure the hell feels like it," Dendy answered.

"Come on." Shell slipped an arm under the driver's legs and another beneath his back. Then he hefted him, walking toward the stagecoach, his eyes going back up South Fork where nothing yet was visible.

He managed to ease Dendy inside the coach and with a lap blanket he found folded in the corner, he fashioned a sling of sorts to keep the driver from rolling onto the floor.

Then Shell moved hurriedly to the box. The horses were weary, but they would have to run. The sun was rising, flashing crimson pennants against the flimsy eastern clouds. A faint violet glow settled against the basin as the first brilliant gleam of gold flared up against the sky, fading the early rising moon.

The remainder of the grade was slow, but once out onto the basin flats Shell was able to let the horses go. They were tired, but they found their pace and he let them have it.

Behind, clouds of red dust billowed into the morning air, and beyond the foothills rose to meet the majestic, purple Rockies. But there was no sign of the bandits and Shell settled into the box, holding his hat as the stage rolled toward Pueblo.

It was another hard day's travel, with Shell not stopping until the horses could run no more. When he let them water at a crossing stream he would walk back up the road or find cover, watching the backtrail, expecting them. But they did not come.

It was an hour after dark the next day when Shell rolled the team into Pueblo. A squat, mostly adobe town there were only a few lights here and there—at a cantina, down at the old Spanish Mission along the river. The Butterfield office was locked up, but Shell rattled on the door until a sleepy head appeared at the upstairs window.

"Go away ... !" the man growled, then he must have seen the stage for there was a flurry of sound as someone scrambled around the room then rushed down the stairs.

"Great Lord!" The door swung open and a man in nightshirt, muttonchop whiskers and gunbelt stood there holding a lantern. He gaped at the coach then at the trail-dirty, tall man before him.

"Get a doctor if you got one," Shell said wearily. "I got Jim Dendy in that coach, and there's a long chance he's still breathin'."

"Jim Dendy . . ." The man turned and called across his shoulder to a boy of twelve or so. "Get Doc Hanvey, Tom! Now!" he shouted.

The Butterfield man followed Shell to the coach and watched as Shelter undid the sling. Dendy's face was a blanched, bloodstreaked mask and the man looked questioningly at Shell who wiped his forehead wearily.

"He's breathin'," Shelter told him. "Shallow, but he's breathin."

Together they picked Dendy up, blanket and all and took him inside where a buxom, red-haired woman stood gawking.

"Get some bandages, soap and water," her husband told her. "Whatever Doc might need."

"He looks . . ." the woman spun away. It was true, he looked most dead and it was slim that Dendy would make it. Shell stood by him until the doctor, a narrow faced man in a blue suit and tie arrived.

Then the weariness told and Shell sagged into a leather covered chair, his rifle beside him, and watched as the doctor snipped away Dendy's shirt, grimacing at the ugly wound.

"You look like you need some coffee."

Shell looked up and nodded his thanks as he took the coffee from the Butterfield man's wife. The Butterfield man reappeared a time later, wearing trousers this time, his hair slicked back with water.

"Name's Webb," he said offering a hand which Shell took. "Mind telling me what happened?"

Briefly, without embellishment Shelter told of the holdup, of recovering the stage, the long ride into Pueblo.

"You just took it back from them?" Webb found that hardly believable.

"That's the long and short of it, I guess," Shell said, finishing his coffee. "A lot of luck was involved."

"But . . . why would you do it? Risk your life for that coach?"

"Dendy needed it," Shell said, nodding toward the sickbed where the doctor still worked. "And, I was riding shotgun. Butterfield paid me to do a job for them, I wanted to do it.

"I think," Shell added with a faint smile, "that I gave 'em their twenty bucks worth."

3.

When Shell woke up it was bright, clear outside his window. He walked stiffly to the window, throwing it open, startling a mockingbird
which had been perched there. It flew off with a
scolding call, swooping toward the cottonwoods
growing along the sun-bright Arkansas River
beyond.

Pueblo ... Pueblo, Colorado. The memory
came slowly. He had slept long and hard the
night before.

Shell washed in the basin and plopped on his hat, swinging his gunbelt around his hips. He was hungry, wanted a shave and a bath. But first off he wanted to look in on Dendy, so he headed up Plaza del More on foot, walking toward the Butterfield office.

There was a lot of activity out in front. Six or seven rough looking men hung around the boardwalk while a hostler finished hitching a team. Shell brushed past a dark-bearded, bulky man in chaps, getting a scowling appraisal in return as he pushed on into the office.

There was a crowd of people inside as well. Webb, three men in dark suits and the city look about them, a man in jeans and a plaid shirt sprawled on the bench, and a tall man with a walrus mustache and a star on his vest.

He glanced up, saw Shell and crossed the room, looking him up and down warily. He stopped nearly nose to nose with Shelter, looking directly into his eyes.

"Morgan?"

"That's right."

"We've got things to talk about. My name's Teerlinck—sheriff here."

"I'd be happy to talk to you," Shell said, although he wasn't crazy about the man's attitude. "First, I've got to see how Dendy is."

"He's alive," Teerlinck said gruffly.

"I'd like to see him for myself." Shell stepped around the sheriff and walked to where Webb stood, watching. "Where's Jim Dandy?"

Webb looked across Shell's shoulder to the

sheriff who nodded. "Second door," Webb told him.

Shell walked down the hallway, finding the open door. The doctor was not there, but Webb's wife was, folding up some spare bandages. Dendy was propped up on two pillows, his face ashen, bloodless.

Yet his eyes flickered open at the sound of Shell's footsteps and he produced a wan smile, lifting a hand.

The sheriff had come in behind Shelter and he stood in the doorway silently.

Shell sat on a chair at bedside and tipped back his hat. "You gonna show 'em, Dendy?"

"I'll make it. With a little luck. And it's thanks to you, Shell."

The sheriff shifted impatiently in the doorway and Dendy's eyes flickered there. "What's he want?"

"He didn't say. Investigatin', I suppose."

"I can tell you what I want, Mister Morgan," the sheriff said plainly. He walked across the floor, bootheels clicking. "The same thing Butterfield Stage Co. want—the gold shipment."

"Gone, was it?" Shell asked. "I figured as much."

"Don't tell me you didn't even look!" Teerlinck scoffed.

"Truth is, I didn't. I was more concerned about our skins. When they didn't come followin', I figured they had unloaded it, though."

"Did they?" Teerlinck's lined face was set, solemn.

"What's that mean?" Shell demanded.

"It means no one knows what happened out there but you. Suppose that gold was still on the coach when you found it. Just suppose you decided to unload it somewhere out there and go back for it later, claiming it had been stolen."

"Then I'd be a thief," Shell said in a tight voice. "But I'm not."

"That's easy to say."

Shell came to his feet, jaw clenched. "I don't like the sound of this. If you think I took it, follow me when I leave Pueblo—I'll not be ridin' north, Teerlinck."

"Who says you're ridin' anywhere until this is settled?"

"You're locking me up!"

"The hell!" It was Dendy who spoke, his voice hollow, weak. "Lock him up and you can lock me up too, Sheriff. Shell saved Butterfield a stage, a team and a driver."

"But lost the gold shipment." Teerlinck was persistent.

"*We* lost it," Dendy said. He coughed, violently. "If you lock Morgan up you'll have to carry me down to that jail as well. I won't put up with this."

Teerlinck waved a hand in disgust, knowing that Dendy meant it, and knowing how it would look to carry a badly wounded man to jail. Especially if it was Dendy—the man was a local hero of sorts. But Morgan . . . that was a different story. Just where the hell had he come from? What was he up to?

"I'll be speaking to you later," Teerlinck told Shell. The sheriff spun on his heel and walked out the door.

"He always like that?" Shell asked.

"He's desperate. Butterfield's raisin' hell with him," Dendy answered. "They told me this mornin' that another stage got hit down south."

"South?" Shell frowned. Then it couldn't be the same gang . . . unless it was a very large, well organized crowd. The usual pattern from what Shell understood was to hit a stage, hideout in the mountains or in Mexico until the money was gone, then strike again.

"I don't think Teerlinck's a bad man, Shell. He's just worried for his badge. He was tryin' to shake something loose somewhere—anything."

"You're probably right." Shell stood, tugging his hat down. "Anyway, don't you worry about it. Rest up."

"You going to be hanging around town?"

"No," Shell shook his head, "not unless they make me. I've a long ride ahead of me."

"Well . . ." Dendy lifted a weak hand. "Thanks, then. Ride with both eyes open and another on the backtrail."

Shell took Dendy's hand and shook it. Then he walked out into the Butterfield lobby where men were milling around. One of those gents in the dark suits was talking to three of those rough-looking cowboys. Shell couldn't hear what he was saying across the room, but he was being most emphatic.

"What's up?" Shell asked Webb.

Webb glanced around to find the tall man leaning on the counter, blue-gray eyes curious.

"They're beefing up the security. There'll be a shotgun inside of every Butterfield coach until this business is stopped.

He crossed his forearms on the counter and asked Shell, "Want a job?" At Shell's surprise he added, "I think Teerlinck's on the wrong trail with you, Morgan."

"He is. But no thanks on the job. I've done my turn and got through with all my parts still hung together. I wouldn't want to go through it again. Besides," he said, "I'm riding."

"So I hear. Into Apache country. Way things are down south, you'd be a hell of a lot safer with Butterfield."

Shell smiled. It was true—from what they said. He had heard some men in the hotel talking about this Thumb, the Chiricahua renegade. Every settler south of Fort Thomas had been run out or was forted up, expecting the Apache.

Teerlinck was near the front door and he motioned to Shell who shook his head and walked through the busy lobby.

"Still like to talk to you," the sheriff said.

"All right."

The morning had grown warm. Passing horses stirred up the dust in the streets as Shell walked with Teerlinck to the sheriff's office. A white adobe building with iron bars in the windows—unique for that area where an old tool shed was often used for the town jail—it had a sturdy plank door, strapped with black iron.

Teerlinck turned the key in the door and let Shell in.

"Sit down, Morgan." The sheriff took off his hat, wiped back his stringy brown hair and sat to his desk, propping a boot up. "Why don't you tell me all about it, one more time."

Slowly Shell went through it, trying to leave out no detail which might help, yet it was little enough he could tell.

"You never saw one of their faces?"

"No. They were hidden when they hit us. It was dark the time I hit them back."

Teerlinck's expression teetered between disbelief and resigned disgust. When Shell was through the sheriff sat tapping his fingers on the desk top, studying Shelter.

"Hell of a tale," he said finally. "Tell me, Morgan—" he leaned forward, fingers interlaced, "just how did you come to work for Butterfield? Walk in off the street did you?"

"That's about it."

"Now you're quitting."

"I am."

Teerlinck nodded. A fly droned across the empty room, and the sheriff's eyes lifted, following it. Suddenly he stood, slapping the desk.

"I hear you're riding south. Mexico?"

"No. I've some business, that's all."

"What sort of business?"

"Private business," Shell smiled. Teerlinck chewed on his mustache tip, shaking his head. He was getting nowhere, and no matter what suspicions he held, he could see that there was no proof for any of them.

"All right." He waved a hand.

"That's it?" Shell asked. The sheriff nodded and he stood.

"That's it, Morgan, but I'll tell you something—don't come back through Pueblo. I don't like you and there's something that don't ring right with you. Nobody in his right mind, no honest man would be riding toward that border area just now. Not alone."

"You said that was all."

"It's all, damnit," Teerlinck shouted. He spun around in his chair, turning his back to Shell who walked from the office into the bright, clear sunlight.

Maybe, he thought, as he walked back uptown, the sheriff was right about one thing. No sane man would ride into that hornets' nest of Chiricahua raiders just now. But Shell had a vengeance in him that was stronger than sanity. He wanted Sergeant Plum, wanted the murderer badly.

He wasn't going to let any Apache beat him to that scalp.

Shell made a deal on a horse—a stocky, deep-chested gray with a blaze on his forehead, and a bay gelding with some age on him for a pack animal.

The Mexican lady at the store filled his order for beans, flour, coffee and salt. Meat he figured to pot shoot. By noon he was on the road south and west, heading for that New Mexico Territory border, the wind stirring the long grass, quail bobbing up out of the grass as they ran from the approaching horseman, the long ranks of pines flooding the mountainsides with deep green velvet.

Spring melt trickled across the valleys in tiny, cold rivulets and the wild flowers had begun to crop up—blue columbine and splashes of scarlet trumpet dotted the hillsides.

A bull elk lifted his head, displaying a massive rack of antlers before bounding off into the timber. It was altogether silent and beautiful—the only sounds the melodic song of a meadowlark, the soft whooshing of the gray's hooves through the spring grass, the wind rattling boughs together in the timber.

Altogether beautiful . . . as long as he did not contemplate the blood which lay behind . . . and ahead.

Instead Shell concentrated his thoughts on beauty, that of the wild country, and now and again of Linda, or Starlight who had made that long winter sweet and warm. Back there—a lifetime ago.

Shell made camp in a small wooded park where the water seeped from a wall of smooth gray granite, ponding for the horses before running down onto the flatlands.

He had his coffee boiling, groundsheet rolled out when he noticed it. The sky was flushed with orange, rapidly fading to darkness as he happened to glance up and pick up twin tendrils of white smoke wisping skyward.

Indians? He dismissed that thought immediately. The Chiricahua had not been sighted this far north; besides the fires were much too large. As a Ute had told him: White men build a large fire and sit away from it; Indians build a small fire and sit close.

The thought also crossed his mind that Teerlinck might be trailing him, still believing Shell could lead him to the stolen gold or to the gang's hideout. Yet that seemed unlikely as well.

Nevertheless it was something to consider. Shell sat cross-legged, sipping his coffee as the last color faded from the sky, watching that smoke.

Morning found him trailing southward once more, the land gradually flattening and becoming drier, although the winter runoff still flowed through the seasonal streams and the grass from the recent rains was lush, plentiful for the horses.

Dos Picos was another week down the trail. A hard edged, flat town, the first he came to on the New Mexico side. A resident red hound glanced up from the center of the main street as Shell trekked into town.

There was a fountain in the center of town where four streets met and Shell stopped, washing his face, cooling his head as two tiny, naked Mexican boys splashed around.

Glancing around he noticed the general store, and needing some supplies he walked over, leading the gray and the pack horse. It would take a while, he saw immediately. There were four wagons drawn up beside the store in an alley. Oxen-drawn, they were new and well built, yet the sides were of four inch planking, the ax-letrees solid oak, banded with iron. They seemed awful heavy for any long travelling—those oxen must have been earning their keep.

Shell tied up at the rail, loosening his cinches. A man with a dark, brushed suit and an odd white collar watched from the ribbon of shade along the boardwalk as Morgan stepped up and moved to the door of the general store.

It looked like a Pilgrim meeting.

There was a bunch of men in those black suits and hats and their women, wearing black with white aprons and caps. They milled around talking in low voices about the goods, quietly standing in line to pay for their purchases. Shell scratched his head and stepped on down to the end of the counter where the jeans and flannel shirts were stacked in neat bales.

Those folks, whoever they were, apparently had no interest in these clothes, nor in the knives, ammunition and such. Shell was able to help himself without elbowing anyone.

"That be all?"

Shell looked up to find a woman of middle years, a hesitant smile, watching from behind the counter.

"Have you got any whetstones? A small one."

"Certainly," she replied. "Under the counter." She bent down and opened a cabinet, showing Shell what she had. "I'm afraid you'll have to stand in line with those folks," she told him as Shell fished for his money.

"All right. Who are they, anyway?"

"Quakers. Decent folks, I guess, but folks won't leave 'em alone up where they come from, so they're movin'."

Shell picked up his purchases and walked to the back of the line. The Quakers were buying mostly food stuffs—dried fruit, flour and bacon. Here and there a man held a shovel or pick.

A tall man in Quaker garb turned to Shell. A straight-shouldered man with iron gray hair and a matching, close cropped mustache he told him, "Thou may take thy packages ahead of us, stranger, if thou will."

"No, thanks," Shell responded. "I reckon I've as much time as you have."

"Only the Lord knows," the man said, "how long a time is given thee."

Shell nodded, shrugging to himself. He idly watched the Quakers move around the store. A strapping kid of eighteen or so picked through a barrel of axe handles. A woman with a girl child in tow looked the blankets over, wagging her head.

Two cowboys, local men it seemed, shouldered through the door and surveyed the crowd with disgust. The taller one, the one in the checked shirt, seemed to have been drinking. He stood unsteadily, muttering something to the other one, a slick looking kid who wore a gun like he fancied himself with it.

Slick turned around, nodding his head as if to go, but his partner grabbed his arm. Shell heard him say plainly.

"The hell with 'em!"

The big Quaker kid who had been at the axe handles had to move the door to get out of the corner and he did so, nudging the cowboy.

"I beg thy pardon," the kid said, lifting his hat. "I did not see thee."

But the tall man wouldn't let it drop. He took the Quaker by the shirt front and growled.

"I'll wring *thy* neck, you damned Quaker!"

The kid had an axe handle in his hand and Shell stood hipshot, watching curiously, expecting the kid to heft that piece of hickory. Instead he answered. "I do beg thy pardon."

The man who had spoken to Shell took a step out of line. "Friend," he called. "The young man has apologized to thee. Do thou let him alone."

Shell stood silently, head cocked curiously. Slowly it began to dawn on him. He had heard it said once before about the Quakers, but he had hardly believed it then—they wouldn't fight no matter the provocation. Maybe the cowboys knew that as well, because they were sure pushing it.

As slick leaned against the door, watching, his partner walked the Quaker kid backward, shoving him hard so that he crashed into a table filled with bolts of cloth. The kid slid to the ground and got up dusting his pants off.

"You! Grover, get out of here with your trouble," the storekeeper shouted. But Grover waved a hand.

"Keep your shirt on Trout. This is between me and this Thee and Thou'er."

The kid had gotten up and standing there dumbly he looked toward the others. Grover reared back and hit him, square on the mouth and the kid staggered back, blood streaming from his mouth. He touched it and looked at it, not understanding.

"I have apologized to thee," he said.

"You'll apologize again," Grover said. "On your knees." He moved eyeball to eyeball with the kid. "You folks like spendin' time on your knees, don't you? You get down on your knees, boy and apologize!" Grover took the kid's wrist and squeezed it, turning it hard, bringing a groan of pain from the Quaker's lips.

"Leave the boy alone," the man beside Shell said. He spread his hands, pleading. "He has done thee no harm."

"I beg thee!" a woman cried out, her hands clenched together.

Shelter Morgan frowned, sighed and touched the man beside him on the shoulder. "Would you hold my goods?"

"Certainly, but . . ." the man took them absently.

Shell turned and walked across the room and Slick's eyes flickered snake-like to him.

"You get up," Shell told the kid quietly. "Go on over there."

"Wait a minute!" Grover shouted, moving a step nearer to Morgan. "Just who the hell are you? He goes when I'm through with him."

"Go on, kid," Shell said, slapping his broad back.

"Maybe you didn't hear me," Grover said slowly.

"Oh, I heard you, I just don't care much what you say," Shell answered.

"No?" Grover's face was ugly with rage. He was drunk. Now that Shell was near him he could smell the raw whisky on the man. Slick still lounged in the doorway, his hand dangling near his fancy gun. "Are you with them?" the man asked derisively, lifting a finger to the Quakers.

"That's right. I'm one of them. With one difference—I got teeth, cowboy. If you don't want a sample, get on out of here. Quietly. Now!"

"You can go to . . ." Grover swung from the floor, but it was a long time arriving and Shell had moved at the same time. Drawing his Colt he slammed it against Grover's skull, cutting a deep gash, putting out the cowboy's lights.

As Grover slumped to the floor, Shell spun toward Slick. The second man had been planning to draw, thinking on it, but now Shell had taken his thunder with that one rapid move.

Slick's hand was on his gun butt, but he was looking down that .44 bore and he didn't like it, that was easy enough to see.

"Throw it away. Over there," Shell told him. Slick hesitated, but Shell eared back the hammer on the big blue Colt and that decided it for him. Gingerly Slick drew his own pistol from his holster and slid it across the floor.

Grover was sitting up now, clutching his head, moaning.

"Get him the hell out of here," Shell told Slick.

"If I see you again . . ." Slick muttered, hefting his friend by the armpits.

It'll be the last time," Shell promised. "Now get out of here before I really lose my temper with . . . thou."

Slick dragged the man through the door, sparing one black look for Morgan. Shell watched a moment longer, then holstered his gun.

He felt a tug at his shirt.

"Thee."

"What?" Shell turned to find himself facing the blackest, most alluring eyes he had ever seen. They were set in the face of a beautiful young woman whose gingham dress only accentuated the full, upthrust breasts, the voluptuous hips of a sensuous creature.

"You said 'Before I lose my temper with thou'. You should have said 'thee'," she said with a suppressed smile which caused the tip of her nose to turn down. She stood expectantly before Shell, blinking those long lashes.

"I'll remember next time," he told her.

"Good." Then she unfurled a blue parasol and swished past him, going to the front door, sparing one last, over the shoulder glance at Shelter Morgan.

"Thy goods," the iron-haired man said, handing Shell his jeans, bullets and whetstone. That was all he said, and from the set of the Quaker's mouth, Shell could tell he was none too pleased with what had transpired.

"I just couldn't stand watchin' the boy get slapped around," Shell told him.

"Those men would have been repaid in God's good time. It is not man's prerogative to take the administration of justice into his own hands."

Well, that settled that. The man turned his back on Shell and moved to the counter to pay for his purchases. Shell stood frowning for a moment, trying to figure out if a feeling of righteousness made up for a busted head or not. He guessed it depends on how you look at things—assuming you can't have both.

For himself he had grown fond of all his body parts, and favored keeping them intact and in working order until the judgement day.

"Thanks. They would have wrecked the store," the storekeeper said as Shell took his turn at the counter. "Grover, he's all right as long as he don't drink. But he always drinks. Christ man—now you watch out for him. He's the brooding kind and he fancies that gun."

"I'll stay alert, thanks. I appreciate the gratitude too. All I got for my trouble was a grammar lesson and a mite of preaching," Shell said, slipping the gold double-eagle onto the counter.

The storekeeper laughed. "They're strange folks, them Quakers. Good, honest as the day is long, but they're rigid in their ways. Can't see 'em trailing through to Arizona," he said, shaking his head as he handed Shell's change back.

"They'll be all right," Shell guessed. "There's plenty of 'em. If they got weapons enough . . ."

"Don't you see," the storekeeper said, "they

don't have a gun among 'em. If they did, they wouldn't use it. They're a trustin' people—trustin' the Lord to get 'em through Thumb and his Chiricahua.''

Shell turned, watching as the last of the Quakers left the store, two men carrying four sacks across their shoulders.

"Well, maybe they'll be lucky," he said.

"Maybe." Trout shrugged doubtfully and closed the register drawer. He leaned across the counter, still shaking his head. "Tell you the truth, mister, it seemed a shame to even sell them those supplies. Like I was encouraging them. Being like they are," he sighed, stretching his arms overhead, "I guess they would have gone on, food or none, though."

Shell scooped up his purchases and walked out. It was hot, sun-bright on the street. A swirling dust devil picked up some loose sand and leaf litter, moving it down the street a ways before dropping it.

He packed up his supplies, looking up and down the empty street, hoping for a second look at the young, dark-eyed woman. But there was no sign of her.

Who was she, anyway? Surely she couldn't have been with the Quakers—if she was, she shouldn't be. That figure would take a man's breath away. It was enough to turn a preacher dumb, the way she moved those hips.

The Quakers were loading their wagons in the alleyway as Shell led his horses upstreet. If they noticed him, they gave no indication of it. To their way of thinking what Shell had done was every bit as bad as what Grover and Christman had pulled.

It was hot, a dry wind out of the east. Shell was not much of a drinking man, but he decided a beer was called for, so he walked to the cantina, tying up the gray. Dusting off, he walked inside.

It was hot in there as well, but dark. Shell found a place at the bar, looking around the room as he sipped his beer. About half the folks were Mexicans. A couple of Indians sat alone at a far table, playing cards silently. A cowboy slept in a chair against the wall.

"Busy," Shell commented to the round faced bartender who shrugged.

"Too damned hot. Come nightfall they liven up." He pointed to a neat round hole in the wall behind the bar. "Last night."

Shell heard the saloon door open, saw a streak of light fall across the dark, scarred wood of the bar, but he paid it no mind until the hostile, familiar voice at his shoulder said,

"I got my gun back, Reb."

Shell turned slowly, his beer mug still in hand. Christman, the gunhand from the store stood there, an evil gleam in his eyes. He had his gun, all right. And he had it out, cocked and levelled on Shelter Morgan.

4.

The cowboy who had apparently been asleep across the way suddenly got to his feet, grabbed his hat and walked out of the cantina. Two of the Mexicans did the same, slipping out of a side door. Shell took it all in from the corners of his eyes as he stood watching Christman standing before him, the ear of that Colt drawn back, ready.

"You boys were askin' for it over there," Shelter told him. "Cool it off now, Christman. I'll buy you a beer."

"It's not that easy," the kid said, knowing he had the upper hand. Lew Christman was quick on the shoot anyway, and with Shelter's gun snugly in its holster, he couldn't help pressing it.

"You made me back down," Christman said savagely. "And I don't like it. I never backed down to no man."

"Then you got some learnin' to do," Shelter told him frankly. "There's things worth fightin' for, maybe worth dyin' for. Stung pride ain't one of 'em."

"Maybe not." Christman agreed. "But I'm not thinkin' of dyin' right now." He laughed then, a raw, ugly laugh. But the laugh broke off in his throat as a voice behind him said:

"Maybe you should be thinking about it."

Shell's eyes flickered. A man in a gray suit, not more than thirty, with a string tie and a line of dark mustache stood behind Christman, and he had his gun out.

"Don't turn around," the stranger warned Christman. "Just drop that gun."

Well, you could see the pain in Christman's eyes, see that it pained him to give up that gun for the second time in the same day without making a fight of it. You could also see that he read the steel in the stranger's voice and he had no wish to die foolishly. He dropped the gun and Shell picked it up.

"I don't think you're old enough to be playin' with these things yet," he said softly. Then he turned, deliberately popped the cartridges from the cylinder, letting them spill out onto the sawdust covered floor of the cantina. Then, with a polite nod to Christman, he held the Colt by the barrel and dropped it into the brass spittoon at his feet.

The color just washed out of Christman's face. A man at the back of the saloon laughed out loud and Christman, shaking with rage warned, "I'll never forget this, partner. I'll track you, and when I find you, I'll shoot you where you stand."

"Christman," Shell replied, "I'm going to give it to you straight. You've given me every provocation for taking you apart. But I peg you for a kid trying to live up to his own idea of what a tough man should be. I also think you got some brains in that thick skull of yours. Let this sink in—you come tracking me . . . ever, and I'll give you just what you're beggin' for."

Shell finished his beer then, slapping a silver dollar down on the bar. He stepped around Christman who was still standing there, grinding his teeth together, and walked out onto the boardwalk. The man in the gray suit was waiting.

"I appreciate it," Shell told him. "I don't know if he would have pulled that trigger or not, but he was making noises like he would."

"He's a big man in town," the stranger replied. "I guess he hated to have you dull his shine."

"You'd better watch yourself too," Shell advised the man. "You've got to be on his list."

"I won't lose any sleep," the stranger shrugged. "Like you, I'm moving on."

"Oh?" Shell had moved to his gray. He tightened the cinch and glanced up.

"I'm with the Quakers," the man said. "My name's Earl Bentley."

"Bentley." Shell took his hand. With the Quakers was he?

"I know what you're thinking," Bentley said with a smile. "No—I'm not a Quaker. Mind walking a ways with me?" he suggested.

"Sure." Shell unlooped the reins of the gray and walked along uptown, leading his animals.

"We're up from Arizona," Bentley told him, "drove a herd of cattle through to Denver. The miners are a good market just now. But," he said heavily, "comes time to go back home and our hands developed cold feet—family obligations, desires to see California . . ."

"Thumb."

"That's right," Bentley told him. They were around the corner from where the Quakers' wagons were and Bentley stopped. "They wanted no part of the Chiricahua. Hell, I don't blame them," he shrugged. "They had a long drive under their belts, they'd been paid off. Who would want to turn around and chance that desert with Thumb rampaging."

"You're doing it."

"We have no choice. It's our spread. It's not much, but we're building. Slowly. We wished the cowboys well and watched them walk away. Then we found out about this Quaker party, and we asked to travel with them, figuring there's strength in numbers."

"Unarmed numbers?"

"Maybe Thumb won't realize that," Bentley said with a concerned frown. "Anyway, we had little choice."

"You keep saying 'we'. Who exactly are you including?" Shell wanted to know.

"Just me and my sister, Drusilla."

"Drusilla?" Shell repeated.

"That's the name my parents gave me," a voice behind him said. He turned to find her watching with those big black eyes, her parasol resting on her shoulder. The girl from the general store.

"Pleased . . ." Shell touched his hat, his eyes going irresistibly to her breasts, those fluid hips. "I'm Shelter Morgan."

"Shelter." She waved those long lashes at him again and Shell felt the blood stirring in him.

"I'm pleased to have met you both," Shell said. "But now, if you'll . . ."

"We want you to join us," Earl Bentley said abruptly, and Shell laughed at first, but the man wasn't kidding and the smile slipped from his lips.

"Join?" He looked from Drusilla to Earl and back again. "You can't be serious."

"Quite serious. You are riding toward the border, aren't you.?"

"I am," Shell admitted, "but with a bunch of greenhorn Quakers . . .!"

"Listen!" Earl interrupted. "How well do you know that desert, Morgan? Because a man who doesn't know it well could die within a hundred miles. Lack of water, sand storms, sudden flash floods . . . Thumb would be the least of your worries if you don't know that desert, believe me."

Shell was silent, pondering. He knew nothing of it, of course, but for what Abe Turpin had sketched out for him. Yet traveling with a bunch of Quakers!

"We know that country," Earl Bentley insisted. "We can get you through if anyone can. Now you may be thinking that you can move faster alone, without these wagons. But moving alone won't help you, Morgan. Thumb will find you either way, unless you're shot through with luck."

"At least this way," Drusilla said, "we'd have your guns and Earl's together."

It made sense, but Shell was hesitant. He was not gregarious by nature, had always preferred travelling alone, fighting alone, trusting to no one else's mistakes or whims. Yet it made sense in a way . . .

"You ever hear of a man named Virgil Plum?" Shell asked suddenly.

Drusilla and her brother exchanged glances then Earl slowly nodded.

"I know him. He's a neighbor of ours, down along Carizo."

"A neighbor?"

"Yes," Drusilla said. "Although we rarely see him. He's a sour, solitary man."

"Shelter was thinking harder now. The Bentleys not only knew the desert, they knew where Virgil Plum was hiding out. Now it might be that Shell could travel quicker alone than with the Quakers, but his path would be less true. There were several points for travelling with the wagon train . . . his eyes shifted again to Drusilla who smiled sweetly and took a deep breath which lifted her breasts. Those long lashes blinked again, and Shell was decided.

"All right," he agreed. "If the Quakers will have me."

"They'll have you. Maybe they won't like it, but they won't refuse a man. I'll speak to Elder Donne."

Elder Donne, as it turned out, was the gray haired man Shell had spoken to at the store. He looked Shell up and down and told him, "Thou art not our kind, Mister Morgan. I do believe that thy guns will bring us to sin. But, come thou with us."

The elder walked away, seeing to his oxen, and Earl slapped Shell's back in parting.

"Mister Morgan?"

Shell turned to see the kid who had taken the beating. His square face was puffed some. A lick of pale hair dropped across his forehead from beneath his black, wide-brimmed hat.

"I am James Thurmond. And I didst appreciate what thou hast done for me. I stand behind the rules and ways of our people, of the Lord of the Friends—for Friends is what we call ourselves, not Quakers—yet thy heart was in the right place when thou didst help. For that I thank thee then."

"I appreciate it," Shell said with a smile.

Drusilla had reappeared, wearing a bonnet and apron, and Shell told her—"I might cut their religion, but that talk . . . !"

"You get used to it," Drusilla replied with a smile.

"Maybe." Shell scratched his head, watching James Thurmond loading a wagon.

A young Quaker woman walked past and Shell's eyes followed her a way. Stately, long legged, she had a pretty face.

"That's not for you," Drusilla said teasingly.

"I don't know," Shell replied, "you know them Quakers don't fight you."

"What makes you think I'd fight?" Drusilla asked. She got on tip-toes and grazed Shell's throat with her soft warm lips, her scent filling his nostrils.

"I don't think Elder Donne would be much in favor of that either," Earl said, walking up to them. He glanced at his sister, then told Shell:

"I guess we'll be rolling within the hour. If you want to ride in our wagon, it's all right."

"No thanks," Shell answered. "I appreciate the offer, but I'm too used to the saddle."

"Okay," Earl shrugged. "If you change your mind, drift on by."

"You could have ridden with us." Drusilla said as Earl wandered on. "With me."

"That seems a mite dangerous," Shell told her. Those black eyes watched him, a teasing sparkle in them.

"Why?" she asked innocently. "I'm a good driver."

Shell smiled. "I'll ride, thanks. But maybe we could have supper together tonight."

"I'd be hurt if you didn't eat with us," Drusilla replied. They had reached her wagon and she stood, hand resting on the wheel beside her. "You never did say . . . where did you meet Virgil Plum?"

"Plum? We were in the army together," Shell said as casually as possible. Drusilla's eyes flickered at that, it seemed, for the briefest possible moment, then assumed a happy innocence.

"He's not a very nice man," was all she said, and Shell did not answer.

"They're rolling!" Earl called, climbing up on the wagon seat from the opposite side. Shelter helped Drusilla make the first step and he stood back, watching her tie her bonnet down tightly as Earl moved the team out, Shell's pack horse tied on behind their wagon.

They trailed out of Dos Picos taking a southwestern course toward La Cima. The mountains they kept on their right hand side, the Rio Puerco on their left, staying with the river as long as possible.

"Drink every time we stop," Earl told Shell, "and remember how that cool water tastes. After we turn west that's all you'll have—the memory."

The land was drier. Away from the river there was little growth, only scattered mesquite and smoketrees. The mountains seemed as barren, gray, lifeless through the low haze. The wagons rolled on easily. The second day a wheel broke on

77

a Quaker's rig, but that was repaired in a couple of hours. The nights were cool, star bright, silent with only the whisper of the wind across the earth.

Shell, riding out alone as was his custom now, cut sign on the fifth day and he told Earl. "A dozen ponies, all unshod, maybe a day old."

"Could be whites. It's a ways between blacksmith shops out here."

"Could be," Shell answered, but neither of them believed it.

From then on Shell worked a pattern. Come sunup he drank his coffee, fueled the fire for the others and saddled up. He rode a long loop ahead of the wagon train then, eyes alert for sign. As morning grew on, Shell rode back to meet the approaching train, stopping for lunch with Drusilla and Earl before continuing his loop, circling in back of the train.

How much good any of it did he did not know. At least any attacking force would be likely to strike at him first, giving the others warning. The Quakers seemed to prefer it that way too. They weren't cool to Shell, but obviously his guns made them uncomfortable.

Day by day they drifted southward, following the river, but there would be a decision to be made, and it was Elder Donne who made it.

"The river has succored us this far. Now we must leave its comfort. Fill thou every water barrel, every sack and can, bottle. Fill thou thine own stomachs and those of thine animals."

They would try it now then, striking west

toward the mountains, across barren sands and rocky, broken ground where none but the Chiricahua and the sidewinder lived, where water was scarce, distant and uncertain.

"With luck," Earl told Shell, "we can find water this time of year along the Gallinas Pass. There should be spring run-off." He lifted his dark eyes as he sketched the terrain in the sand, "yet that water's uncertain. It roars down the mountainside canyons with the force of locomotives at times, moving horse sized boulders. Yet on the flats, that water will disappear into the sands before it's flowed a hundred yards."

"Donne knows all this?" Shell asked, looking toward the river where the elder directed the filling of the water barrels.

"I've told him," Earl said. "But I don't think it really sank in. It doesn't until you've tried it out there. The way Donne looks at it, his God will see him through to Fort Bowie anyway."

"I hope he's right," Shell admitted.

It was a somber, beautiful land. Long stretches of amber sands, broken mesas, towering red buttes and spires. Then the Gallinas Mountains, standing ten thousand feet tall, ghostly through the haze as if the ancient desert spirits still haunted their forbidding reaches. A beautiful, raw land—and a deadly one.

Shell walked to the Bentley wagon, finding Drusilla gone. Probably she had taken their water bags to the river. Shell went to the rear of the prairie schooner and shifted some goods, looking for his own spare canteen.

It caught his eye, and he frowned.

The planking of the wagon bed was neatly fitted, nailed down to the heavy frame. What had caught his eye was the row of bright nailheads near the tailgate. All of the other nails were rusted. But not these.

Sweeping the dust aside he saw where a section had been cut out, and recently by the color of the wood along the line. Looking around, he saw no one.

Shell took his Bowie from the sheath and pried gently, raising a section of planking. He lifted it just enough to slide his hand under the wood. Searching, he found something. A canvas sack, and inside . . . he withdrew his hand and looked at the mint-new double eagle in it.

Shell pursed his lips, glanced around to make sure no one was looking, then slid the coin back, estimating by the size of the sack how much gold was in there. It was plenty. Perhaps fifty-thousand dollars.

He eased the plank down and tapped the nails into place with the butt of his pistol, sifting some dust over the section before replacing the goods.

"Shell?"

He turned, canteen in hands, to find Drusilla watching him, and for a moment there was a hard, searching look in those deep black eyes.

"I've got to fill up too," he said casually, swinging the canteen over his shoulder. He walked by Drusilla, and she stood watching him, hands on hips as he sauntered toward the river, whistling a broken little tune.

Earl slipped up beside his sister, watching Shell's back. "What is it?" he asked.

"He found the gold."

"You sure?"

"Yes," she said, turning to face Earl. Drusilla bit her lip and watched as her brother thought it over.

"It might have been a mistake bringing Mister Morgan along," Earl said finally. "A very big mistake."

5.

They rolled on. Climbing out of bed while the stars were still bright in the chill sky, starting long before the fierce daytime temperatures could build, draining the strength of man and beast alike.

The far mountains were their landmark, their goal. Yet day after day, the Gallinas which appeared so near in the clear desert air, seemed to withdraw as if nature itself were mocking their effort.

The going became sandy, the heavy Quaker wagons rolling with the greatest difficulty across the washes and cholla studded flats.

Time after time the wagons sunk up to their axles, the oxen bawling terribly. Then a second team had to be unhitched to draw the sunken wagon out, everyone pushing, pulling and sweltering beneath the merciless sun.

"You're too damned heavy," Shell finally told Donne who flinched at the mild curse. "I've seen plows, barrels of nails . . ."

"And we shall need them for our planting, our building once the new home is reached."

"Elder, you ain't gonna reach that new land. Not if you don't lighten up. That wagon there has a printing press in it!"

"And that we shall need to spread the word to the heathens . . ." he eyed Shell coldly, "of whom there are apparently many in this savage land."

With that Donne turned away and left Shell to look after him, wondering at these folks' faith . . . or their delusions. "You're talking to stone," Earl said behind them.

"I reckon." Shell shook his head, smiled and ran a hand over his sweat-dampened hair before replacing his hat. Earl handed him a canteen and Shell took it, frowning. He took a short drink of the tepid water and asked, "How's the water supply?"

"Not good. You'd be surprised how much an ox can drink when he's thirsty."

Besides a brackish pond of water left from the last rain they had come across the day before, water had been non-existent since turning away from Rio Puerco. Each wagon carried two fifty-gallon barrels strapped to the side, but as Earl said, the oxen could soak that up in no time at all.

If they drank too much too quickly, the water was bound to run out; if the oxen were not given the water they needed it all became academic. Without the oxen they were doomed.

They were deep into Apache territory now, but it hardly entered their thoughts. It was the sun, the sand which dominated their consciousness.

The oxen trudged on, out of habit, desperation. The sun glared down, parching lips, drying the perspiration as quickly as it formed on their bodies. Shell's eyes were red-rimmed, rough as if sand filled them when he blinked. His lips were split open, his shirt white with the salt of perspiration.

Now and then he glanced up to the mountains, those mocking distant mountains where it should be cool, where there should be water . . . the horse beneath him moved on mechanically.

The oxen had been put on half-ration by Elder Donne, but the gray was given all he wanted to drink. Shell had no intention of letting that horse die under him.

Through the glare of the white sun Shell saw Drusilla wave a hand, and he wondered at her. She was holding up well, better than most. True she had her bonnet, the morning shade of the wagon canvas, but that was little enough—there was no way of escaping the blazing fire in the sky, the reflected heat of the sands.

Only at night was there any relief. Even when they wandered dry-mouthed around the circle of wagons, or fell to a fatigued sleep. It stayed hot until well past midnight, then the temperature dropped suddenly, bringing a frozen early morning.

Shell hunched over the tiny fire, drinking his coffee. How far had they come? And how far was there to go? Always in his thoughts were the Apache. The Quakers, who trusted to divine intervention did not worry themselves with thoughts of Thumb; but Shell knew that wherever the Apache warlord was, it would only be a matter of time before he came across the wagon train.

On that broad, empty desert, nothing could move without being seen for miles. Nothing but the solitary desert sheep and the Chiricahua.

Earl sat by the fire, poking it to life with a twig.

"Feel like riding?" he said.

Shell looked up, face fire-bright, eyes curious. "Riding where?"

"Out there." Earl nodded toward the far mountains, invisible against the ink of the night. "I've been talking to the elder."

"Water?" Shell guessed.

"That's right." Earl moved around the fire to squat beside Shell, as he did so the firelight picked up the pearl-handled Colt tucked into Earl Bentley's belt. "We're running this game mighty close," he told Shell.

"If we could lighten those wagons . . ."

"Donne won't do it," Earl interrupted. "I've suggested it three times at least. What we need is to be sure we will find water once we reach the mountains." He sketched a diagram in the sand before Shell.

"There's two passes in our line of travel, Shell. Turnbull and the old Spanish Fork. Turnbull has plenty of water at times. There's a cluster of tinajas—stone basins hollowed out by water which most of the year hold sweet water."

"Not always?"

"Nothing is always out here," Earl told him. "The wind erases landmarks. Water is the most precious, short-lived commodity in the desert. It's a long drive up Turnbull. A rough steep trail. If there's no water in the tinajas at the crest . . . the oxen will never make it down the other side."

"What then?" Shell asked.

"We'd try Spanish Fork. It might be we'd come up dry there as well. Then we'll all be looking to our hole cards. But the Spanish Fork water is from a seep, slow-moving, but reliable, most times. The trouble is, of course, with that kind of water source there wouldn't be enough for all the stock. Some would die," Earl said, "but some would make it."

"You'd prefer Turnbull then. If the tinajas are full, and the water's good."

"That's it. But we won't know until we get there. Unless we scout Turnbull out."

"All right," Shell agreed readily. He was the logical man to ride ahead; the only one with a saddle horse. Yet for a brief moment he had his doubts. Was it that Earl wanted the water scouted or that he wanted Shell out of the way?

Riding alone to Turnbull, suppose the tinajas, as they called them, were dry? And suppose the wagons had taken Spanish Fork . . .? But he had no real reasons for those suspicions. What was it that did not ring true about Earl Bentley?

The man had saved his life. True, they had a sizeable amount of gold, but they had supposedly just sold a herd of cattle. How large a herd had it been—that had not been mentioned, nor had Shell asked. He only knew that fifty-thousand in gold was enough to start the wheel's turning in anyone's mind.

"Lay it all out for me, Earl," he said. "I'll ride out at dawn."

They spent an hour scratching rough diagrams in the sand, Earl explaining exactly where the water tanks should be located. Then Shell kicked out the fire and shouldered his bedroll, walking a ways from the camp, through the cool darkness.

The hand fell on his shoulder before he saw it coming.

"Shell?"

He turned to her in the darkness and she clung to him. Drusilla ran her hands up and down his back, clenching his hips, drawing him to her.

"You're riding out tomorrow?" she asked.

"Yes."

"I don't want you to." She was near in the night, her woman smell ripe, her hands searching.

"It's best," Shell replied. It was dark but for the distant stars, the last reddish glow of a campfire inside the circle of wagons.

"Can I kiss you goodbye," Drusilla asked, and her voice was breathy, deep.

"You'd better," he answered. Her hair was down, glossy and dark as the night itself across her shoulders. Shell bent his head and she kissed him hungrily, holding his head so that he could not pull away if he wanted to.

Her open mouth was wet, warm and Shell felt his body tingle as she kissed his mouth, throat, ears, breathing softly into them. She made a small, deep sound of satisfaction in her throat and then gasped.

"It won't be enough to kiss you goodbye," she decided. Her hands went to his crotch, fumbling with the buttons of his jeans, his belt.

"Here," Shell whispered. His hands met hers and he unbuttoned his jeans, letting his growing erection free. She took it with both hands, running searching fingers down to his thigh, then back along the shaft.

"You're a stallion!" Drusilla whispered, her full mouth going to his lips again wildly. She whispered into his ear. "I want that . . . now."

Shell had not been brought up to argue with a lady and he wasn't about to do so now.

"Hold me up," Drusilla said. Shell did so and Drusilla hoisted her skirt. There was nothing under it.

Or rather there was something. She brushed it against Shell. Her eyes glittered in the starlight as his probing fingers touched her soft bush and dove inside, finding her hot, soft, ready.

"Now . . ." Drusilla threw her arms around Shell's neck and lifted her legs, locking them around Shell's hips. It was lady's choice, it seemed, and it was up to Shell to work this out. He lifted her hips a bit, touching her soft inner thighs, spreading her lips until he felt the tip of his pulsing erection touch her soft inner flesh.

Drusilla's head rolled back, her teeth showed white in the meager starlight and she slid slowly on, her legs still locked around Shell's waist. She scooted slowly forward, working her pelvis in gentle circles.

Shell's hands, beneath her skirt, supported her. He kneaded the firm flesh of her buttocks, his fingers feeling the alternate tensing and relaxing of her muscles as she eased his full length inside. His fingers were damp now with the juices of her body, and she began a slow, pulsating thrust.

"You're so . . . huge!" she said in an exultant, joyous whisper. She quivered and rolled, her legs vise-like around Shell, her throat filled with a low, distant humming sound as she slowly milked his erection.

She was still then, just for a moment, sliding slowly back. Then Drusilla's body began trembling and she thrust herself wildly against Shell, uncontrollably trembling, gasping; and as she reached the wild throes of her climax, Shell gripped her buttocks savagely, driving it home as Drusilla's fingers raked his back, his shoulders.

She clung to him like an exhausted child, her eyes bright, heart wildly racing and Shell felt the continuing waves of contractions inside of her, felt the exhaustion growing to new eagerness as she thrust her tongue into his ear, kissed his throat savagely.

"Again. Please do me again, Shell . . . I want it. I need it. You're such a man . . ."

"Drusilla!" They heard Earl's voice calling from the wagons.

"Again," she panted. "Fuck me again. All night."

"Drusilla."

"Earl's calling."

"Let him call. I want you inside of me. All over me . . ."

"Drusilla!" The voice was nearer and Shell glanced around. He could see Earl's shadow now.

"No. Not now," he said reluctantly. Jokingly he added, "I'm liable to lose my balance anyway."

"I don't care." She bit at his lip, let a hand slip down his abdomen to where his still hard shaft entered her own soft flesh. "Again . . ."

"No." He said softly, but firmly. Reluctantly Drusilla slid off of him and Shell buttoned his jeans. She stood, her head against his shoulder, rubbing the bulge in his pants.

"All right," she sighed. Now she too could see Earl moving closer and she silently cursed her brother, the desert. "But when you come back . . . make sure you do come back, Shelter," she said, searching his face.

"I will. Now," he smiled, and she kissed him again, running off towards her brother.

Shell walked off a little farther and unrolled his soogan. Then he lay in bed a long while, watching the distant starts, catching a glimpse of a brilliant meteor shower, listening to the far off howl of a lone coyote.

If it was a coyote. He rolled over and slept, the Winchester in his big fist as the night grew colder, emptier.

6.

Shell rolled out early. Shivering in the pre-dawn hour, he coaxed the campfire to life and threw a handful of coffee into the pot to boil. Slapping his arms, he rocked on his heels, studying the stars for a minute.

"Mister Morgan?"

Shell looked up to find James Thurmond, collar turned up to the chill. The Quaker kid had a burlap bag in his hand.

"Mornin'," Shell grunted. The coffee was boiling over, hissing into the fire, and he folded a cloth, grasping the pot handle. He poured himself a cup and, noticing the Quaker was still there, offered him some.

"No. I thank thee."

But the kid did not leave. He stood there like an overgrown puppy dog and Shell sat on his heels, sipping his boiling, black coffee.

"Was there something . . .?" Shell asked finally.

"I am to go with thee," Thurmond said with what seemed a touch of pride.

"You're to go . . .?" Shell nearly choked on the scalding coffee. "Go where, son?"

"With thee to scout the water holes. The elder hast . . ."

"Tell the elder, no!" Shell said sharply. "Absolutely no."

"I couldst never," James Thurmond said, his open face concerned. "The elder hast advised me to travel with thee. So I must."

"Look, kid," Shell said, rising, "it's going to be a rugged trip. Dangerous, believe me. You don't even have a horse."

"Elder Donne wishes me to take thy spare pony."

"You tell Elder Donne . . .!" Shell sputtered, shrugged and sat down again, finishing the coffee as he studied the square, honest boy before him. "Can you ride? I mean really ride?"

"I have ridden," Thurmond said proudly.

The camp was stirring to life. It was time to be going. "I'm not too crazy about this idea," Shell told the kid flatly.

"The elder expected as much. He told me thou wouldst rant, thou wouldst rage, but I must be steadfast."

Shell shook his head in wonderment. There was only one possible reason for Donne sending the kid along—he wasn't sure he could count on Shelter to return. Yet that did not aggravate him as much as the high-handedness of it.

But there was logic on Donne's side. It was his train, and as wagon master, he had unwritten authority to do as he wished. Yet Shelter had been a loner most of his life. He rode alone, fought alone, not wishing to worry about anyone else when trouble started. Now he would have a worry—this hound-eyed kid who carried no gun.

"I only got one saddle," Shell told him.

"I shall ride bareback," Thurmond said agreeably, his mouth forming a grin now that he knew he had won. "And I shall follow thy instructions."

"Fill up the canteens," Shell ordered, tossing them to the kid. "Then meet me at the Bentley wagon."

"Yes, sir," Thurmond said, and happily he ran off toward the water barrel. Shell mumbled a lengthy curse and threw the dregs of his coffee against the fire to hiss and steam.

At first light they rode out of camp, Shell leading, riding his gray toward the black bulk of the mountains. Thurmond hung back a way, making work out of riding the bay bareback. He was not used to it, and the horse which Shelter used for a pack animal, had not been ridden in a long while—if ever.

The bay wandered where it wished, balking, standing still at times as the kid flailed wildly at it, hands, legs and hat, trying to keep pace with the easy stepping gray.

Shell halted on a small pebbly rise just as the first crimson arrows of dawn pierced the sheer clouds to the east. Thurmond drew up apologetically beside him.

"The animal is new to me. If thou will be patient with my efforts . . . I will reward thee with my diligence."

Shell was mopping his forehead with his scarf. It was already over a hundred, it seemed, the dry winds off the mountains brisk.

"Do what you can," Shell said.

"Thou wouldst . . ." the kid began, but Shelter cut him off with a sharp motion and an angry, frustrated sigh.

"Kid . . . James," he said pleadingly. "I don't want you riding with me. And you're not doing much of it. But we'll be together for most of three days, I reckon. Can we make a bargain?"

"A bargain, sir?"

It would be easier on me if . . . you could talk like a damned human being while we're out!"

"Thou meanest . . ."

"You know what I mean." Shell glanced toward the horizon where the wagons showed only as black specks rolling toward them. "You're breaking my ears, son. I know it's your way. But if you could find it in your heart . . .?"

Thurmond sat woodenly on his pony's back, his face revealing frank astonishment. "I wouldst try, sir, but . . . "

"That's the elder," Shell nodded toward the distant wagons. "He won't hear you, and I won't tell."

"If it would make your journey smoother . . . I can attempt to forget my speech patterns . . . for just this little time. If it will please thee. You . . . "

"It would, son. Bless you, it surely would please me." Shell tugged his hat lower. "Let's get a gettin' before the sun gets higher."

The going was slow. The trail Elder Donne hoped to used for his wagons was rough on a horse. Drift sand and a kind of black, glassy lava which was slick, dangerous to moving stock obstructed the travel.

At mid day nothing moved out on the desert flats. The jackrabbits hunched in the shade of the scattered greasewood, barely finding the energy to lope away as Shell and Thurmond approached, their horses dragging.

"Let's give 'em a rest," Shelter suggested finally.

Thurmond nodded, wiping his red face, and they slid from the horses' backs, walking them through the deeper sand. The mountains now bulked over them, shouldering the blue white skies. Rugged, empty pyramids of gray earth and red stone, they offered no promise of respite.

Yet in late afternoon they brought the relief of an early shade. Riding again, Shell steered the gray through a wide thicket of nopal cactus. Green, abundant, it was a tortuous, barbed thicket where nothing lived but the scuttling lizards, the cautious kangaroo rats and the scorpions which proliferated after sundown.

It was a deadly, venomous land. Yet as the sun faded behind the Gallinas, the land took on a nearly hypnotic beauty. The amber sands, shifting eternally, took on a violet hue in the shadows, a brilliant rose in the sunlight.

Shell sat on a flat rock in the Gallinas foothills, a dry wash running away from them toward the flats where the long shadows had awakened, stretching out long, questing arms.

A flight of doves winged across the purpling sky, seeking some distant feeding ground, some watering place only they knew. The wind shivered the low chaparral in the bone-dry canyons, and away in the distance a towering red butte caught the last golden ray of sunlight at its pinnacle before the defiant light was absorbed by twilight.

A first, diamond-bright star hung pendant in the eastern skies. Thurmond, sitting quietly beside Shell watched as it blinked on.

"It's a proud land," he said reverently.

"Proud and unforgiving," Shell replied softly. "She gives man no quarter."

Thurmond glanced at the lanky, blond-haired man, perhaps surprised by this meditative quality. He knew nothing of Shelter Morgan, he reflected. Other than the fact the man had fought for him. Sinfully, perhaps, but with no motive other than to help. Who was this Shelter Morgan? Where did he travel.?

He asked him, but Shell only responded, rather roughly: "Scratch up some of that broken brush. We'll start a chow fire."

Thurmond put his wide, black hat on and did as he was told, scrabbling over the rough canyon, gathering ancient, weather-grayed manzanita, scrub oak and the skeletons of some long-dead nopal for the fire.

Shell was hunched over his pack, digging out utensils, coffee and beef jerky when Thurmond returned, his arms loaded down with fuel.

They ate quietly, hunched near the small fire as darkness closed over the canyon. When they were through, Shell kicked sand over the fire and sat in the darkness, drinking a last cup of coffee as he studied the far desert.

"Why are you riding south with us?" James Thurmond asked again.

Shell glanced at him. The kid was only an indistinct shadow in the night. He could not make out his features, see the kid's expression as he told him—"I'm riding to kill a man."

The pause which followed was long, thoughtful. Thurmond spoke again finally, asking Shell, "You're not a lawman?"

"No. Not a lawman. There's no law out here to do my work for me. I've tried before. In Washington I asked the government to find this man and the others like him. They wouldn't, couldn't . . .

"There's no witnesses to their crime, you see."

Shell told him. "They killed them all. But me."

Shell turned up his collar and took a sip of the cooling coffee. Thurmond was silent, and Shell could guess the Quaker's thoughts. He felt obligated, somehow, to justify it to the kid, and so he tried.

"They killed three friends of mine, James. Betrayed our cause and killed their own soldiers. It was back in the war . . . a long while back, it seems now. At times it seems like it was only yesterday."

"You're poisoning yourself with it," Thurmond offered, and Shell did not disagree. "Spending your life in such a way. You have said there is no law to support you, Morgan. But there is always His law. The Lord will judge these men when they appear before Him."

"I'm just makin' sure they get delivered to Him quick as possible," Shell said. Thurmond did not respond to that. How could he? All of his thinking, from birth, had taught that what Shelter Morgan was doing was wrong, sinful.

But he had not seem them die.

Shell put his cup away and rolled up in his blankets, listening to the night. It was an hour later, perhaps, when he heard the cry of the coyotes once more—this time it was not so far off.

And it was the following morning as they rolled from their beds, shaking their boots to make sure no scorpion had taken its temporary home there, that Shell again saw the smoke.

It was not the Quakers. They were farther

north, distant, Another party travelling this wasteland through the Apache territory? It gave a man reason to ponder.

7.

It was all of the next morning and most of the afternoon before they crested the storm-damaged trail into Turnbull Pass. The temperature had dropped, blessedly, as they climbed the nearly eight thousand feet, but outside of an occasional, struggling cedar, a wind-flagged pine, the land was every bit as desolate as it was on the desert flats.

Above them there seemed to be some timber, maybe some grass, in the sheer, slanted high country, but no man would ever walk among it. The road up had been a nightmare on horseback, and although Shell and James Thurmond had taken the time to roll some of the flood-washed boulders aside and clear some long-dead skeletons of trees from the trail, still it was borderline if the wagons could crawl up that snaking road or not.

From the crest they could look down on the western desert. If anything it was emptier, more forbidding than that on the eastern side of the Gallinas and Shell cursed in wonderment, wiping his perspiration-soaked forehead with his scarf.

"As long as no one thought we were in good shape once we cleared the mountains . . . look at it, James."

The Quaker, hat in hand stared out at the shimmering white distances, where nothing visible grew for mile upon mile. A trick of the sunlight and reflecting sands caused a shimmering, bluish mirage to appear square in the middle of it all. The illusion of water, one of nature's cruel hoaxes.

Nothing moved out on the desert. All of the world was desolate, barren as a moonscape.

The tinajas, from Earl's description should be up a narrow feeder canyon half a mile farther on, and they rode that way, eyes lifting to the whitish, barren mountain slopes. The tanks, if they were there, would be high on the rim. Probably the water would have to be hand-carried down. It would be hard going, hazardous, but it was the only way if the stock were to be saved.

Shell's eyes searched the naked rock, the clinging dry vines which in the late spring would become hanging gardens of brilliant red monkey flowers. A skeleton-leafed paloverde tree tilted crazily from the cliff face.

"See anything?" he asked Thurmond.

"No. But then I don't know what I'm looking for."

"We're going to have to climb up there," Shell said with resignation. The breeze was stiff now, the cliff face sheer, liable to crumble under any weight. But there was no other way—the tinajas could not be identified from below.

Thurmond stepped from the horse and stood beside Shell. "I believe I can climb it," the kid said.

"Stay with the horses," Shell decided. "I'll have a look." He drew on his gloves and put his hat on the pommel of his saddle. "Hand me my rope, will you?" Shell said.

Thurmond unhooked the lariat from his side of the saddle, and handed it over to Shell who held it coiled, eyeing the cliff for a long minute, trying to decide on the best course.

Then he slipped the rope around his neck and under one armpit, walking toward the cliff, still studying it, looking for handholds of any kind.

It was a hundred feet up. The rock ancient, crumbling. There was a small chute of sorts where the rim of the cliff had given way, beginning a small landslide, and Shell decided to try it there.

The rock was loose, unsettled, but the climb

would not be so steep there. Taking a deep breath he unbuckled his Colt, handing it to Thurmond who took it as if it were a snake, and began slowly upward, testing each handhold and projection before putting his weight on them.

The wind had picked up, buffeting Shell's back as he inched ahead, the sun in his eyes when he looked up to search a crevice or struggle toward a new foothold. A fair-sized thumb of rock jutted out, offering a hold . . . but that too was illusion. As Shell grasped it, tested it, and trusted his weight to it, the rock broke off and he slid dangerously down, saving himself only by wedging a fist into a root-formed crack.

The jolt nearly tore his arm from his socket and he glanced down, panting, to where Thurmond stood looking up with undisguised concern.

There was nothing to do but try again and Shelter crept upward, grasping the exposed roots of a manzanita, finding an inch-wide toe hold which was just enough to lift him to a tiny ledge where his hands found purchase.

As he scrambled up, another rockslide started a trickle of rocks and dust down the chute, and Shell held his breath. But the ledge held and he was able to stand cautiously and with a single secure handhold he dragged himself up, and over onto the cap of the cliff.

He stood unsteadily, dusting himself off. Thurmond was waving up to him and Shell waved back before turning, surveying the mountainside laid out before him.

He was on a small shelf, perhaps a hundred acres, no more, which rimmed the higher, broken peaks with a crescent of pale green.

Looking to the east he could make out, or believed he could, the wagon train through a shifting haze. The water tanks, if he had been properly informed, would be at about his present level, and to the north.

He strode the shelf, rope still coiled over his neck, seeing nothing but a long dead pinyon pine, the days-old tracks of a cougar.

Shell circled an outcropping, inching along a narrow ledge and found a larger, but drier valley where the grass lay in a brown blanket across the rocky earth. To his right several huge slabs of basaltic rock had slid from the mountain crest. As neatly layered as if they had been sliced purposely, they were nearly fifty feet high, half again as wide.

None of this looked right, and he walked ahead, walking where possibly no man had before, before coming to a dead end in a high rising, three-sided canyon.

He had missed the tanks then—somehow. He reversed his course, taking a lower, eyebrow trail back toward the south. Now he saw signs of water—deep green buffalo grass, insects humming past his ear, the droppings of a desert bighorn sheep.

A wind twisted pinyon pine jutted from the cliff side, like wrought-iron against the pale earth. Day had begun to fade, and that quickened Shelter's steps. He had no wish to be caught in unfamiliar territory after sundown.

He slid down a rocky wash and clambered up the other side. His shadow was long before him on the overgrown trail. The white faced mountains took on a pale orange sheen.

And then he was there.

Coming around a tight bend in the trail, he suddenly found the tanks. Water trickled from high on the mountain, filling a broad, shallow pond which eons had cut into the solid rock. Overflowing, the water ran into a oval shaped, apparently deeper tank some twenty feet below. Shell tasted the water. It was cold, sweet.

Looking around he could see that he was not far from where he had climbed up onto the shelf. Earl's description had been accurate, it was only that the original path had broken down, slid away into the gorge, so that now the only access was the circuitous route Shelter had taken.

The shadows crossed and recrossed, blending together to form dark blankets against the earth and Shell turned, retracing his path hurriedly, racing the dying sun.

Finally he found the chute once again, although there was little more than twilight remaining and the canyon itself was black, empty. Where was Thurmond?

Peering over, he could not spot the Quaker.

He took his rope and secured it around a large boulder, tying a stiff buntline hitch in the new hemp. Then he straightened, tested the rope and moved toward the rim.

There was a flash of color, the whisper of moving feet and Shell felt the body strike him with full impact. He clung to the rope, felt it slither through his hand, and he grabbed desperately at the rim's edge as he was knocked over the lip of the shelf, his head spinning.

Shell glanced up, saw the boot arcing toward him and swung his head aside just enough. The boot grazed his jaw, but Shell was able to retain his grip on the rope, and now he clawed upward, standing on the edge of the shelf, facing the Chiricahua brave as sundown washed to darkness.

The Chiricahua was naked to the waist, his long black hair tied flat beneath a red head-band. He wore the calf-high Apache moccasin-boots and a sullen, challenging expression.

The knife in his hand caught the last brilliant gleam of sunlight as he crouched, watching the tall blond man before him.

Shell's hand went to the scabbard on the back of his belt and came up with his bowie. He held it turned up, easy in his hand as the Indian tried a mild, feinting slash, measuring his man.

The knife whooshed past Shell's belly and Shell's own knife darted out, striking at the Chiricahua's arm. The Apache, eyes seemingly amused, swung to one side and again feinted.

This was a better move and Shell took the feint, and as he stepped aside, the Chiricahua moved in, his knife hand going high, his free arm taking Shell at the wrist.

Morgan's forearm went up instantly, and he managed to step inside the vicious downward arc

107

of the blade. The Apache slashed out again, but Shelter twisted free, his own knife parrying the blade of the Indian.

Cool perspiration clung to Shell. The dust from their movements filled his nostrils. Warily he watched the Indian.

A deep chested, black-eyed man, there was a terrible scar across his chest. His nose had obviously been broken once; it wandered aimlessly across his tanned, rugged face.

Shell backed away a step, but halted as he felt the edge of the cliff near him. The Apache shuffled forward a step and then suddenly turned and kicked out with a foot which was aimed at Shell's crotch, but Shell had seen it coming and as the Apache's foot caught him a grazing blow, Shell took a lunge forward and with an upward movement took the Inian's leg and forced the motion of the kick to continue.

The Apache lost his balance as Shell flipped him and he landed with a grunt on his back. Shell moved in, but before he could land on top of the man, the Apache, cat-quick in his movements, spun aside and to his feet.

He lunged again at Shell, and his knife caught flesh across his abdomen, tearing Shelter's shirt open as a razor thin trickle of blood began to flow.

Overconfident now the brave moved in again, and again he thrust downward. But Shell was ready for that one, and he caught the Apache's hand with his own, bending it backward at the wrist as the two men stood face to face on the lone mountain top, muscle straining against muscle in a deadly contest.

Shell could feel his strength giving, could see the knife of the Apache slowly descending. The Apache's eyes glistened with satisfaction. But he had not won it yet.

Morgan brought up a stiff knee to the Chiricahua's groin and as the man went limp with dazed pain, Shell collapsed on his back, legs thrust up. His feet caught the tumbling Indian in the abdomen, and Shell threw him over.

Panting, the brave scrambled for his knife as Shell spun. Now each was cautious and they circled slowly, the only sounds the ragged breathing of the two warriors.

It was Shelter who made the first move now. Going in low, he ripped up the razor's edge of his bowie, and the brave jerked his head back as Shell's knife point carved a chunk of meat out of the warrior's cheek.

Angry now, determined, the Apache stalked, whipping out with his legs, trying to trip Shell. That did not work and it angered him farther, the blood from his facial wound trickling onto his cheek.

For a brief moment Shell saw the Indian's muscles relax, and from some instinct bred in combat, he knew what would be coming.

The Indian had relaxed for only the briefest moment, then he bunched his muscles, diving at Shell like some big cat, his blade driving downward. But the brave had moved impatiently. Perhaps he had underestimated his adversary. Perhaps he had slipped as he lunged, but his movement was hasty, wild.

Shell side-stepped and drove upward, the full force of his shoulder and chest muscles behind the savage, telling blow. He felt the bowie sink to the hilt in the Apache's abdomen, felt the hot, sticky blood flow across his hand, the twisting, frantic action of the Chiricahua's body as he tried desperately to fight back, to evade the blade, but it was too late.

The man fell, got to his hands and knees and then stood, hands empty, Shell's bowie protruding from the ugly gash beneath the breast bone. The Chiricahua put both bloody hands on the haft of Shell's knife, but he could not pull it out.

His legs had begun a trembling, and his face seemed bloodless, his eyes stunned, uncomprehending. He took a half step forward, a rubbery, mechanical movement. Then he half-nodded, perhaps in a gesture of respect. Then he staggered, tripped and toppled over backward, falling over the lip of the ledge, slamming against the rocks of the chute until he came to rest on the canyon floor far below.

Shakily Shell walked to the edge of the bench, holding his stomach where a little blood still trickled from the shallow gash. He sat down for a moment, letting the wobble go out of his legs. He tore his shirt farther open and examined the wound more closely. It was utterly superficial—yet close, very close. An inch deeper would disembowel a man. The Apache had been very strong, very good with a knife.

Were there others around on that mountain? Or had he been a lone warrior, perhaps seeking water too? It was possible he had been posted to watch the tinajas.

Shell stood and picked up his rope; leaning far out, he walked himself down the face of the chute, showering sand and gravel.

It was dark, cool, silent in the canyon. Shell brushed himself off and walked to where the Indian lay, face up, eyes white, wide. He pulled his bowie free, wiping it clean on the brave's leggings before tucking it away in the sheath at the back of his belt.

He heard gravel crunching under a boothel and he spun, his hand automatically going to his knife once again.

James Thurmond stood there, his face collapsed into pained confusion. His eyes went from Shelter to the dead man at his feet and back.

"He's . . . dead," Thurmond said as if he needed to say it before such a thing could be believed. "You killed him."

"He came at me," Shell said. "I killed him before he could kill me. I favor living."

Shell walked past Thurmond who stood gawking, looking sickly pale. Shell was afraid the kid might throw up.

He took his pistol off the saddle horn of the gray and buckled it on. "Let's ride out of here, Thurmond. There might be more around, though it seems not."

Thurmond turned slowly, his face ashen in the

starlight. He nodded, dazed, and clambered onto the bay's back, following Shell back through the long canyon.

They used the campsite of the night before. There the long canyon walls rose up on three sides and below the world dropped away toward the flat, empty desert. It would be difficult for anything, man or light-footed beast to move to them.

Nevertheless Shell was worried. The Chiricahua had spotted them. Perhaps the brave he had killed had been a lookout whose duty was to flash a signal—smoke or mirror signal—to the warlord, Thumb, if the wagon train did come by way of Turnbull . . . that was just a guess.

What Shell *knew* was that someone, woman, chief, brother, friend would know where this Apache had been, and worry when he did not return. That would bring others.

James Thurmond stared into the fire like a man who had been shattered. Perhaps the kid had never seen a corpse before. His folks held the taking of life the greatest sin, the unforgiveable crime.

Despite himself, Shell liked the kid. Liked him a lot, Shell himself had spent three years killing, three years seeing men die. It was never easy, but he preferred seeing his enemy lying dead to the thought of his own corpse rotting in the sun.

The Quakers, to Shell's way of thinking, were dreamers. They had decided how the world ought to be and were shocked when harsh, violent reality intruded. Shell had seen a different world. A world where the strong survived, where those who win are those who are right. Where soft words never turned away wrath.

"It wasn't something I wanted to do," he told the Quaker across the cold fire. "I never seen the man before. Maybe where he comes from he's thought of as a good man, a kind father . . . but he come at me, Thurmond.

"I never saw him before. He wanted to kill me. I didn't want to die."

That was as plain as Shell could put it; if the kid didn't understand, well—he never would. Shell rolled up in his blanket and glancing over he saw that Thurmond still sat, hunched over like he had been, staring into the distance.

The stars were brilliant diamonds spattered against the sky. The wind drifted down the long canyons. Shell listened as he lay there, on that rocky slope.

The coyote no longer howled.

Elder Donne stood at the head of his wagons, his face red with the heat, his eyes piercing, head held proudly.

Shelter rode that gray in slowly. It was weary, the day an umbrella of white heat, the sand searing. James Thurmond followed some ways back, the bay's head bobbing with exhaustion.

Shell slipped from the saddle and accepted a canteen from Earl Bentley with thanks. Drusilla had rushed forward, but stopped abruptly, leaning against a wagon, eyes bright with an undefined emotion.

Shelter drank deeply from the canteen. The

water was warm, but his every cell soaked it up eagerly. He replaced the cap carefully and through blistered lips said, "There's plentiful water at Turnbull."

"Accessible?" Elder Donne wanted to know.

"It'll have to be hand transported. In barrels from the high tanks. But it's there. Cold, sweet."

James Thurmond had gotten from his horse and he staggered forward like a man in a dream. He politely asked for the water, politely drank it, keeping himself in check.

"And what of the savages?" Donne asked abruptly. "Hast thou word of them?"

James Thurmond's head came around sharply. His eyes locked with those of Shelter Morgan. The kid watched, expectantly. Shell wiped his hatband out and planted his hat on his head.

"We saw some sign," he told the elder.

"They may be up there?" Donne said.

"They may be . . . like I say, we saw sign."

Shell's eyes flashed to those of Thurmond. Donne saw it and he asked the Quaker kid: "There was evidence of the savages, James?"

"We saw evidence, sir," James Thurmond said, then he turned suddenly and walked away. Donne studied Shell with those cutting eyes and nodded slowly.

"How many hours to Spanish Fork, Mister Bentley?" he asked Earl.

"Too many. I'd say if Shell found the water, hand carry or not, we'd best take Turnbull."

"And I agree with thee," the Quaker said. He nodded to Shell. "We do thank thee for thy efforts."

114

Earl stood next to Shelter, watching Donne return to his wagon, leading the exhausted train forward. "What was it?" Earl asked.

"You read me that well?" Shell asked.

"You're not that hard," Earl said. He nodded at Morgan's torn shirt, the fresh scab on his belly.

"I had to kill one," Shell said simply.

"A Chiricahua!" Earl turned to watch the wagons plodding past. The elder scrutinized them carefully as his wagon moved out. "If they're up in that pass . . ."

"I think it was just the one, Earl. It's a risk, but what two ways are there? We can have water in Turnbull. If we don't get water, we're all done for."

"That's right. You're right." Earl ran a harried hand through his hair. There had been quite a change in this man since Dos Picos. Dapper, he had seemed then, neatly shaven but for the thin mustache he sported. Now his gray suit was badly wrinkled, his cheeks shaded with dark whiskers. "You know how much of a chance we stand if they hit us there?"

"I know," Shell answered. "And I know how much of a chance we have without water."

"I wish . . ." Earl began, but his voice broke off suddenly and his hand flickered toward the butt of that pearl handled Colt he wore. It was quicker than any draw Shell had ever seen and he flinched as Earl touched off a single shot firing behind Shell, into the sand.

Shelter turned slowly. The snake thrashed

wildly about. A sand colored sidewinder, it was, and its head had been neatly severed by Earl's shot. A stream of hot blood still spurted from the body of the sidewinder, and Shell turned his eyes back to Earl Bentley.

What kind of shooting was that then? The kind any cattleman learns? Maybe in Arizona, but Shell had seen men whip out a handgun and empty it at closer range, trying to kill a rattler. With Bentley it had been draw. Fire, kill. With hardly a thought, no aim, off-handedly.

That was twice. Twice Earl Bentley had saved Shell's bacon with that fancy gun. This time had been different. This time Shell recognized a fast gun, a man of exceptional talent, and he knew that he never wanted to face Drusilla's brother with six-guns.

Why then did the thought nag him that one day it would come to that?

8.

The wagons creaked and jolted upward behind double teams of oxen as the Quakers fought their way up Turnbull Pass—their goal, the revitalizing water which would see them across the wasteland to their new home. It was only their dream which kept them going on. People without a dream would have long since quit, perhaps never begun.

A wagon teetered on the edge of the broken trail, and a wheel broke free as Shelter Morgan watched. The oxen were dragged backward, bawling loudly, their clambering hoofs unable to stop the rig from tumbling over, the driver leaping free as the wagon, oxen and all thundered into the gorge below, breaking into splinters, throwing goods every direction, the panicked, battered oxen lying broken, crippled beneath and beside it as it shivered to a stop far below.

The driver stood shaken beside Shell and Elder Donne.

"It was my plow, my books, my seed," the man said miserably.

"And will we not share with thee, Friend?" Elder Donne asked, putting an arm around the man's shoulders.

The elder looked up sharply. Shelter Morgan had his Winchester in his hands. Below an oxen continued its terrible bleating and Shell's rifle went to his shoulder. He fired twice, the shots echoing up the canyon. The ox lay still.

"You are quick to use that instrument of death," Donne said savagely.

Shell did not answer. Instead he turned on his heel, slipping the Winchester into his saddle boot, yanking the gray's head around more sharply than he had intended as he rode upward, past the struggling Quaker wagons.

"Shell!" Drusilla called out to him, but he did not reply. He rode instead to the head of the canyon where the first of the Quakers had arrived beneath the tinajas.

Earl Bentley was there, a fresh shave on his face. "Going up with me?" Earl asked. He was stripping off his jacket. He folded it and placed it aside while he waited for Shell's answer.

"Sure. The two of us?"

"I've asked young Thurmond up. He's a husky kid, and he'll be a help."

"All right."

Shell loosened the cinches on his horse, ground tethered it and took off his hat. The Colt he left on this time. He might drop it, clog it, but it was better than finding he needed it and had left it hanging on his saddle.

"Figure they're up there?" Earl asked, noticing the pistol.

"No. Do you?" Earl was wearing his fancy Colt behind his belt. Bentley smiled and shook his head.

"I don't travel naked much," he answered.

Thurmond had arrived, hefting two empty fifty-gallon barrels and some more rope. He blinked when he saw Shell, but said nothing.

Shell climbed up first, watching the distances, the canyon where the Quaker wagons still labored as he waited for Earl to scale the cliff.

When he was up, Shell fashioned a sling of rope to haul the barrels up with. Earl, in the meantime, swept the empty, rocky hillside with his eyes. He glanced back impatiently at Shelter.

"You're taking a time with those knots."

"You'd better believe it. A gallon of water goes a mite over eight pounds. When we bring those barrels back we'll have some strain on these lines. We won't be able to fill them all the way up anyway. We'll take what we can handle, move that back and pour it into a standing barrel, then start again."

"You'll make a day's work out of this."

"We will. You haven't seen that country we have to haul the barrels over yet. It's rough stuff, Earl. We'll have earned the water when we get it down."

It was all of that and more. The three of them could only handle about half a barrel at a time. And that was up steep slides, around the narrow trail. They lost one cask, watching with dismay as it burst apart on the rocks below.

"Maybe it can be repaired," Thurmond had said.

"Find the man who can repair that and we'll set him to work on the ox that fell," Shelter said, watching the splintered, shattered barrel.

It was full dark when the last barrel was lowered in Shell's sling to the waiting hands. Earl sagged onto a rock on the lip of the ridge. His hair was damp with sweat. The rising wind rumpled his torn white shirt. He glanced up at Shelter Morgan.

"How about lowering me in that sling? I'm beat."

"Catch your breath," Shell replied. He stood for a moment, mopping his brow, watching the sunset skies.

There it was again. "Still there. Still coming," he muttered.

"What?" Earl looked at him curiously.

Shell lifted a pointing finger toward the east. "There. See that smoke?"

"What about it? Think it's Indians?"

"No. No I don't, but that doesn't make me any more comfortable. There's someone on our trail, has been for days."

"Well," Earl shrugged. "Then they're as crazy as we are."

"Yeah."

Shell watched a moment longer. Who would be trailing them? Or should he ask—who would be trailing Shelter Morgan? That smoke—he had seen it shortly after leaving Pueblo, after that run-in with Sheriff Teerlinck. Teerlinck had pegged Morgan for his man . . . did he still believe it?

There was nothing to go on. Probably it was not the same campfire. But who? Who, on this desert, when every man back to the Rio Grande knew that this was Thumb's desert?

"Ready?" Earl Bentley was eyeing him oddly. He hesitated then asked Shell—"Are you on the run?"

Well, now, he didn't even know *that*. Shell laughed and answered, "I guess we're all running from something."

It was dark on the mountain ledge. Earl answered slowly, "Yeah, I guess so." There was an odd edge to Earl Bentley's voice, but in the darkness Shell could not make out the man's facial expression.

"Let's get on down," Shell said.

They had started no campfires on this night, and the Quakers sat in small circles, silently eating, letting the exhaustion wash out of them.

The oxen appeared wobbly, stunned as Shell crossed the camp, but they had water now—although not as much as they wished for.

Shell found Elder Donne's wagon. A candle burned inside, the canvas was drawn shut. He rapped hard on the wagon bed twice and after a brief, muted word to someone, the elder appeared in shirt sleeves, hatless. His face twisted at the sight of Shelter Morgan.

"I'd like to talk to you," Shell said. It was obvious that the prospect was distasteful to Donne. He did not want to talk to Shelter, to see him. It was a feeling Shell did not like—knowing that this Quaker hated him, but there was nothing to be done about it.

After a moment the elder was back, wearing coat and hat, He stepped down from the wagon to face Shelter in the night.

"What is it?"

"I don't know what your figurin' is, Elder, but if you're plannin' on moving out tomorrow, I think it's a mistake. The animals have drunk, but they're far from recovered. Another few days in the sun could kill them—water or none."

"What art thou suggesting?"

"Stayin' here. We could let the stock have all the water it needed, fill up them barrels again. Here, in the gorge we've got morning shade and afternoon shade. Let the animals have their rest. Let your folks have a rest."

"No." Elder Donne replied immediately. His jaw was set, his eyes hard. "We must reach the new home. The Lord has chosen us and we will not tire in His service."

"You're runnin' your oxen into the ground!" Shell flared up. Beneath all of it—the speakin' of the Lord and all, Shell had the feeling it was just plain stubborness which caused Donne to reject the idea out of hand. Just the fact that Shelter had suggested it. "I've caught a glimpse of that western desert," Shell went on, more calmly. "It's as wide and arid as the eastern. None of us knows where the next water might be."

I have answered thee," Donne said sharply. "Ride out with us tomorrow or stay behind on thy own. More the better for us, to be without thy evil influence." Now what did that mean? The elder explained: "The body of a young Indian man was discovered beneath a pile of rubble from the cliff. He had been murdered. Is this thy 'Indian sign' which thou reported?"

"He attacked me. I knew you wouldn't favor hearing of it."

"A young savage killed. Needlessly. And thou hast corrupted one of ours—young Thurmond stood in thy lie and turned the face of truth from his own."

"He was here," Shell said hotly. "Maybe he saw how it was—saw it wasn't no sin, but a pure act of self-defense. Maybe he ain't so rockheaded, Elder Donne."

"And perhaps," Donne said slowly, biting his words off, "his soul is now lost as thy soul truly must be."

At that he turned and stepped to the tail gate of the wagon. "We travel in the morning," he said before disappearing behind the canvas flap. Shell stood there a minute before turning angrily away.

He bumped right into her.

"Not so rough," Drusilla laughed in a whisper. He put his arms around her, kissing her open, warm mouth. "That's better," she said.

"Better. Not as good as I'd like it," Shell answered. "Let's walk a ways."

"I saw you talking to the elder. What about?"

"He wants to roll out in the morning. I was trying to talk some sense to him. It was no use—like I was the devil whisperin' in his ear."

"He doesn't like you?"

"Well, he don't want to baptize me just yet," Shell said, scratching his ear.

They had come to Drusilla's wagon and she leaned back against the wheel, Shell close to her, feeling the contours of her body against his.

"Don't let it bother you—I like you," Drusilla said. Her lips found his throat, his mouth. "And I've a lot more to offer than Elder Donne."

Shell laughed, but his seriousness returned. "I'm damned worried about it, Drusilla. I don't think the stock is going to make it in this heat. Nor some of the folks—the old ones and the younguns, especially."

"But we will get through?"

This was the first time Shell had seen Drusilla worried, and she seemed deeply worried. "Sure," he told her with a confidence he could not feel. "We'll get to Bowie."

"I . . ." she fingered Shell's shirt front, standing close to him. "If anything should happen to Earl . . . you will take care of me, won't you?"

"Nothin's going to . . ."

"I know. No," she shook her head, looking down momentarily. "Nothing will happen. Of course not. But . . . you would look after me, Shelter? You would take care of me?"

Her eyes were bright, searching. Her hands held his shoulders tightly as she waited his answer.

"Sure," he said with a quick smile. "I'd take care of you, see that you got to Bowie."

"Promise?"

"Of course," Shell said, puzzled. Then with a tip-toe stretch she kissed Shell once again, deeply and turned, going to her wagon. Shelter Morgan stood there, frowning.

Now what was that all about? Sudden panic, fears of being left alone—well there was good reason for it. Good reason for any of them to feel scared from time to time.

Still, it was hard to figure, and Shell found no easy answer for it. It was late, cool, dark. He hefted his bedroll and with a single backward glance at Drusilla's wagon, he walked some ways from the camp and made his bed in a small, protected hollow.

Despite his weariness, sleep was long in coming. Sometime after midnight when the rising moon was glossing the canyon walls Shell sat up suddenly, feeling that someone was watching him, had been approaching.

Yet he saw nothing. When he looked toward

125

the camp he found it still. For just a moment it seemed he saw a shadow moving near the Bentley wagon. But when he blinked it was gone, and all was silent in the camp, the deep, cold gorge.

9.

At dawn they were moving down out of the Gallinas, onto the searing white flats which spread out before them in savage panorama. Nothing grew there. Save the useless, stick-like greasewood, the isolated ocotillo plant—like a bundle of spine-covered coachman's whips, a delicate flame colored flower gracing its tip.

It had been warm at dawn, the temperature rising inexorably as the oxen, heads bobbing with weariness, drew the wagons downward.

Each thousand feet had been telling, and once onto the flats, the temperature had blossomed into furnace-like heat.

If it was a hundred and twenty in the air, it was thirty degrees hotter on the surface of the sand. The stock plodded ahead painfully, in bewilderment.

There was utterly no wind, no sound but the empty of the wagons and they moved across the creaking land. The only living thing they saw hovered in the white skies, circling. The black silhouette of a vulture, stark, forboding.

Shelter had ridden out ahead, looking for a place called Grumman Ford where Earl said there was water—had been a few months ago. Yet a few months under that sun could have reduced the pond to cracked, dry clay, and that was what Shell expected to find.

To the south the land was piled high with huge white dunes. Drifting up the flanks of the chocolate covered mountains, some were a hundred feet high. Ahead the sand gave way to cracked, salt playa.

The remnants of an inland sea, the playas were baked clay, frosted with inches of salt, a desolation where nothing would ever take root, grow. The gray Shell rode moved across the playas, the ancient brine crackling under foot as the sun branded Shell's back, whitened his clothes, burned his neck and hands red.

To reach Bowie it was necessary to skirt the massive dunes, climb yet another range of mountains—the Peloncillos—and somehow, somewhere, find water where there was none . . .

Yet the dunes seemed interminable, and the mountains could not even be seen across the white, baked distances. Shell turned in his saddle, seeing nothing.

He took a small drink of water from his canteen, replaced the cork and swung down from the gray's back, giving the animal a needed rest.

Oddly, he thought of the promise he had made Drusilla—to take care of her, protect her. At that moment Shell felt no confidence in his ability to take care of himself.

He halted the horse and poured a little water into his hat, watching as the gray eagerly thrust its muzzle into it.

"Not enough, is it fella? It'll be a time before we have us enough."

He slapped the horse's neck affectionately and continued on, leading the horse whose neck drooped with weariness. There was no sign of the arroyo—the dry creek which was supposed to point the way to the ponds at Grumman Ford, nor of the red sandstone rocks called Rooster's Comb which jutted up from the sands inexplicably somewhere in the area.

Shell walked on, watching the lone buzzard which still circled in the sky above.

"You know, don't you, you damned devil-bird? You seen enough of us two-legged animals walkin' this desert to know, haven't you?"

The sun was directly overhead. Sweat trickled down Shell's throat and was dried as a rising, hot wind hit him. There was still no sign of the ponds or of any of the landmarks.

Soon he would have to turn around and go back if he did not want to be alone on the desert at night, and he did not.

"A little ways more," he told the gray which pricked up its ears curiously.

Off through the distance he saw it then, or thought he did. The rising heatwaves shimmered and changed perception. But it looked to be Rooster's Comb, and he swung the gray that way.

He was taking a risk now, veering off into a waterless stretch, far from the wagon train, but the need to find the ponds forced it.

The sun was in Shell's eyes, burning them. He squinted against the glare and urged the dragging gray onward. He climbed a low, sandless rise and there they were—the ponds.

He eased the gray down, skirting a patch of jumping cholla. Reeds grew around the rim of the ponds, brown lily pads lay against the cracked mud. The ponds were dry.

There was enough in a murky, stagnant pool for the gray however, and Shelter let it drink, eyes shifting. He walked around the dry ponds as his horse satisfied his thirst, searching the ground.

There it was! The reason the ponds were dry.

It was not only the sun which had emptied them. There, deeply scored in the still damp mud near a clump of reeds were the tracks of a dozen or more ponies. None had worn horse shoes.

Shelter quickly squatted and poked at the mud

with a twig. A dozen Indians. That sign was not more than a day old, either. Any longer and the sun would have baked that clay to red stone.

Shell stood, walking quickly, warily to the horse, eyes probing the distances through the glare of the shimmering sun.

"Let's go," Shell told the gray as he stepped into the saddle. "We're drinking in somebody's back yard."

He met the approaching wagon train ten miles back, as the first of the Quakers to arrive at the campsite was unhitching his rubbery-legged oxen. His wife teetered on the wagon seat, her face waxen. Long shadows stretched under the wagon and Shell rode up to the man.

"See to your wife," he said sharply. "I'll water your damned oxen." The man stared blankly at him out of red-rimmed black eyes. "She's got sunstroke, damnit!"

Elder Donne had walked up and he glared at Shelter. "Running my wagon train again, Morgan?" Donne snapped.

Shell turned stiffly, blue eyes stony.

"Look, Donne. I'm hot, I'm tired. I'll not take any of your preaching now. Not just now!"

Then Shell walked to the water barrels and found the wooden trough the Quaker used to water his stock. He filled the trough to the brim and let the oxen drink, Donne watching him all the while.

The sun lay low on the horizon, spilling out crimson sundown onto the desert. Earl Bentley walked to Shell, his face dust streaked, clothes white with alkali.

"Well?" he wanted to know.

"The water?" Shell shook his head. "It's gone. I saw sign there—a dozen Apaches easy. We're riding into their teeth, Earl."

"Have you spoken to Donne?"

"Not exactly," Shell said.

"We'll have to," Earl said. "If there's no water at Grumman's Ford, we have to swing south. Maybe we can skirt those dunes."

"Maybe," Shelter said doubtfully. And he knew there was no way they were going over them. A wagon and team could disappear in those mountains of sand. "There might be another way."

"Go on," Earl urged him.

"I'm not sure about any of this," Shell said hesitantly. "But I spoke once with a man named Turpin—an old desert rat. He sketched out some of the country west of here for me. Do you know of a place called Wattle Hill?"

"Sure, but there's no water near there. And it's way north, Shell, off the track."

"Turpin said there's water there. A seep high on the north flank of the hill. As far as being off the track goes, Earl, I figure any place we find water ought to be on the track."

"True. We'd still be moving west, I guess we wouldn't lose much . . ."

"We'd be veering away from the Chiricahua, I'm thinking."

"You're sure there's water?" Earl wanted to know.

Shell shook his head. His face was determined, hard. "I'm sure that Turpin says there is. And I'm sure that there's none ahead—none the Apaches haven't drunk."

There was no doubt in Shelter's mind that this was the way they had to go. Convincing Donne was another matter. His eyes hardened at the sight of Shell, and it seemed his ears had turned to stone as well.

"No," he told them flatly. "Our route has been long planned. We have gone over it often. It is the best way, the quickest way."

"It would be if you could make it," Shell said, the blood rising.

Earl rested a calming hand on Shell's shoulder. He spoke softly to Donne explaining.

"Morgan found plenty of Indian sign at Grumman Fort, Elder."

"Indian sign? And did he murder the 'Indian Sign' this time?" Donne demanded caustically.

Shelter turned angrily away. "You talk to him, Earl," he said. Shell walked to the water barrel on a nearby wagon and took a deep drink with the dipper which hung there, startled to see how little was left in that barrel. The splashing, evaporation and the heavy thirst of the oxen had taken their toll.

"Well?"

"Earl walked up to him, shaking his head. "He'll not hear of it. Donne insists his way is the correct one; and he says you know nothing of the desert anyway."

Shell shook his head slowly, looking along the

line of wagons to the purpling empty stretch of desert ahead. "For a man of God," Shell muttered slowly, "Donne's in an all-fired rush toward Hell."

They moved woodenly the following morning. The sun rose abruptly, with hardly a softening flush of dawn, and they scarcely looked at it, as if afraid of acknowledging its very existence.

The oxen plodded dumbly on, white with alkalai, tongues dangling. Now and then one would drop to its knees and the wagon would halt until the animal could be coaxed up, given small amounts of the precious, saving water.

The people were in no better shape. One child cried interminably. Day and night as they rushed into Hell, the sunburned face of Elder Donne turned defiantly to the desert sun as he led them on.

By the second day they had seen some hope— the end of the dunes, yet without a water source it made no difference. Two oxen had died. The child. A pathetic little cross marking the site.

Still Donne pushed westward, south, away from the only known water.

Shell stayed away from the wagons, going in only when it was utterly necessary for water. In defiance of Elder Donne he continued to let his horse drink all it wanted, all it could. The oxen might have been saved if Donne had allowed them the water. Skimping would likely only ruin every chance they did have, putting them all afoot, unable to carry the water which remained.

He cut no more Apache sign, though the

ground they tracked over now was sandy again, likely to hold no hoofprints. Yet he worried about it constantly. They were two armed men against a savage band of renegades.

The third night found them bogged in sand still. Without the strength to make camp, to eat, the Quakers tumbled into their wagons to sleep, leaving the dying oxen hitched. They did not drink—there was no water.

A man had gone under from the sun, running madly across the desert until Shell and Thurmond tackled him and brought him screaming back to the shade of the wagon.

Now it was still. Cooling air brought a faint relief although the sands were still warm. Shell made his bed atop a dune, a little ways from the wagon train.

He watched the matchless beauty of the brilliant stars against an utterly clear sky. Nearer than he had ever seen them, their varied colors bright, true. And he smiled faintly at the irony of such beauty being where man is the most vulnerable, unlikely to indulge his senses with it.

"Are you sleeping?"

Shell's head rolled to find Drusilla there, her night dress sheer, revealing.

"No." he said quietly. "Just tired, like everyone."

"I can't sleep," Drusilla said. She came to him and by the starlight he could see her perfect breasts through the gossamer of her gown.

"It's always either too damned hot or too cold

135

out here, isn't it?" Shell commented.

"Let's not talk about it. Not tonight." Drusilla stood at his feet, and Shell, propped up on one elbow studied her breasts, those full, curved hips, the dark triangle between her thighs.

"All right," he agreed. "What do you want to talk about?"

"Nothing. I don't want to speak, to think, I only want to feel."

She slipped her chemise up over her head and stood there proudly, a hauntingly lovely ghost from out of the sands and Shell flipped his blanket back.

"Get in here," he said. "I promise I won't make you talk."

She smiled, shook her dark hair loose and walked to him. Shell threw his shirt aside and kicked off his pants. Then she was beside him, her soft body against him.

Drusilla lay back and Shell followed her, his lips going to her taut nipples, his hands finding her warm inner thighs. She made a small, animal sound of comfortable expectation, nearly like a cat's purring as Shell kissed the point of her chin, her navel, her breasts in turn.

The starlight was in her eyes, on her body. She lifted her open mouth to his and he met it hungrily, his tongue intertwining with hers as his fingers explored the soft curly bush beneath her smooth, flat abdomen, finding her tiny, hooded shaft hard, throbbing.

He toyed with it as she kissed him more excitedly, and he let a finger dip into the soft depths of her, brushing the tiny pink rose which blossomed there.

Her hand dropped between Shell's legs and he shifted slightly, letting her cradle him in her palm, her fingers digging behind his scrotum, pulling him closer.

He traced tiny figure eights inside of Drusilla, running from deep within her up the quivering clitoris and back again once more into the warm, fluid, widening cavern.

She leaned forward sharply, bit his chest, her hand going to the back of his neck to hold Shell to her as her other hand began an urgent stroking of his pulsing erection. She tried pulling that to her, impaling herself on its warm length, but Shell held back, teasing her.

For just a moment, and then the urgency which was sending tremors through Drusilla's body welled up in Shell and he rolled to her, letting her fingers guide his shaft inside slowly, as she drew him to the hilt, a tiny gasp escaping from her open lips.

Drusilla rocked slowly back and then forward, enjoying the man within her to the fullest. She lifted her knees to allow Shell to penetrate even deeper and she trembled, biting at his ear, her hands running up his back from his hard buttocks to his neck.

Drusilla arched her back, thrusting her pelvis against Shell's and he slipped his hands beneath her, lifting her hips even higher as he went to his knees, hands clenching her smooth buttocks.

His eyes went over her body as she swayed

beneath him. Her mouth was open; she touched her tongue to her lips. Her breasts were flattened slightly now, her nipples taut. Her abdomen was firmly muscled beneath a layer of soft, feminine flesh and it quivered now as Shell lifted her still higher, driving against her warm, sticky crotch.

Her eyes opened, and he saw they were unfocused. She was lost in pleasure's distances and she was aware only with her body, her swaying, demanding body.

Shell drove in to the hilt, and Drusilla moaned, her head thrashing from side to side as he stroked, still supporting her hips, eyes still feasting on her white, star glossed body.

Then she came, a shuddering, convulsive release emptying her body, and Shell followed, driving into her time and again before letting her hips go, pressing flat against her to finish his pulsing climax as she stroked his hips, naked back, thighs, her mouth hungrily snatching at his neck and mouth.

It was then that the shots rang out from the wagon train, thundering across the desert flats in a rumbling, constant volley.

10.

Shelter Morgan flattened out. Beneath him Drusilla squirmed and he put a hand across her mouth in time to silence her cry. Another fusillade of shots echoed up the dunes and the gray tossed its head, broke the ground tether and galloped away.

Shell lay utterly still, Drusilla naked, flat against him, her eyes wide. A piercing, savage scream filled the night air. Still Shell did not move, except to snake his pistol from the nearby holster. He held it cocked beside Drusilla's head, listening to the howls, the screams from beyond the dunes.

Then there was another sound, a slowly building, ferocious sound. Shell could not identify it for a moment, and then he did—the crackling of flames.

A pale yellow light, streaked with red flooded the night sky, shimmering off the white sands. From the corner of his eye Shell saw another shadowy movement. He kept his hand gripped tightly over Drusilla's mouth.

The brave was nearly on top of them, only fifty feet off, perhaps, silhouetted against the fire which he turned to watch.

Perhaps it was the firelight in his eyes which caused him to miss seeing them in the hollow of the dunes, but he turned away and Shell lessened the tension on his trigger.

It was cold and Shell was naked, but his body was filmed with sweat now. The fire flared up hotly, a crimson flag hung against the blackness. And now there was a lot of smoke, trailing off towards the distant mountains.

The shooting had stopped.

So had the screaming, the war cries of the Apaches—it was over. Now Shell knew they would be sacking the wagons, taking scalps, looting bodies.

They lay still until their bodies were cramped, chilled by the night. Still they did not dare move. The fire had burned low, the wash of black, soot-filled smoke drifted for miles around, staining the sands.

It was almost dawn, the first tint of gray coloring the eastern sky before Shell, stiff, chilled, stood and slipped into his jeans. Drusilla lay there, watching him as he pulled his boots on.

"Get up," Shell whispered.

Her black eyes were wide, it almost seemed she could not move. She shook her head. "I don't want to see it."

"Get up!" Shell tossed her sheer night dress to her and he stood, picking up his Winchester.

Slowly she did as she was told, moving woodenly, her fingers trembling violently so that Shell had to button up the gown for her.

Shell turned and headed toward the wagons, but Drusilla hung back. "I don't want to go back there," she repeated, her voice muffled, distant.

"We have to. Staying here won't make it go away," Shell answered. He smiled briefly, and put out a hand. She followed reluctantly, hanging back as Shell moved toward the Quaker train, rifle at the ready. The gray, which had returned, watched warily.

Suddenly he stopped, atop the low dune. Drusilla stopped automatically as well; she was still ten paces back.

"They're gone," he told her, turning his head. But Drusilla could read the pain on Shell's face and she came forward only hesitantly, her eyes turned down to the sand where his tracks were cut into the ash-layered dune.

Shell stood stock-still, rifle in both hands, and he took a deep breath—it was what he had expected to see, what he had seen on other battlefields, in other times, but it was still a savage, gut-wrenching scene, and Shelter had to fight it down.

Drusilla took one look and sagged, holding onto Shell's shoulder until the dizziness passed.

"You want to stay up here?" he asked her.

"No." She shook her head decisively. "I'll go with you."

The wagons had been burned to ash, the oxen slaughtered—one had the haunch butchered roughly off, for meat apparently. The others lay inert, throats slashed, crumpled against the sands, eyes wide in death.

The Quakers were strewn about the ground— some had been shot at close range, others slashed with knives. A yellow-banded arrow protruded from the bloody body of Elder Donne.

Drusilla, still in a daze, her nightdress utterly incongruous, followed Shell through the camp. James Thurmond lay across a dead oxen—his scalp lifted.

Shell shut his eyes—he had liked the kid, and it seemed the kid liked him despite their differences. The charred remains they stood by now were those of the Bentley wagon and Drusilla gripped Shell's arm tightly.

"I can't . . ."

"Then stand here, damnit," Shell said roughly. It was not anger which forced his words, but a frustration, a feeling that all of this could have been avoided by turning north, by showing enough strength of arms that even Thumb would not have dared to attack.

The scorched iron loops which supported the canvas still stood, but little else remained of Drusilla's wagon. Her clothes, trunks, all had been destroyed or sacked and strewn about the ground.

Shell moved to the back of the wagon, searching the white sands. Then he peered inside and beneath the remains of the burned hulk.

Yet he did not see what he expected to find, what he had every reason to find . . . the body of Earl Bentley.

Drusilla's face looked hopefully to him.

"He's not here."

"No." The bay was gone, but the Apaches had probably taken it. Maybe not. Maybe Earl had made his run and gotten caught a ways from the camp. Drusilla brushed by Shell and went to the ash littered bed of her wagon.

"Give me your knife," she said abruptly. Her eyes were glittering.

Shell handed his bowie over and watched silently as Drusilla pried up the wagon bed's hidden compartment. Her hand fished in and came up with a charred canvas sack.

The gold.

She opened the sack and a handful of glittering coin tumbled into her palm. She glanced at Shell triumphantly, those black eyes bright. Then she tucked the coins back into the sack.

"At least they've left that," Drusilla said. Everything else seemed to have gone out of her mind and Shell just stared.

"Let's pack it then, and get going," he urged

143

her. "We'll not find Earl. If he's alive, let him find us."

"Could he . . . make it?"

"Possible," Shell shrugged, although he did not believe it. If he had the bay, if he had water . . . Earl's chances would then be only as poor as those of Shelter Morgan himself.

There were still two hundred rough miles to go. Two hundred waterless, Apache-infested miles with a single horse, a near naked woman and a couple hundred pounds of gold . . . the odds didn't stack right on them making Bowie.

Or even the next hillrise.

But there was nothing to do but go on, to try it, and Shell prepared for it as well as possible, searching the wagons for a scorched water bag which he filled with the sooty remainder in the bottom of a broken cask. He packed the gold on the gray's hip, sat Drusilla in the saddle and moved out, the sun hot in the morning sky, the death-scent still heavy in the air.

The wagons could not have made the dunes. Shell meant to try it with the horse. For one thing it was the shortest path, for another, it meant moving away from Thumb's forces—something they must do if they were to survive.

The dunes were deep, not as deep as the mountainous sands near the Gallinas, but some were stacked fifty feet or better, and there was no footing. For every two steps forward, they slid one back, Shell going onto his knees at times as the gray bucked forward, sliding down the far sides.

It was exhausting, killing beneath that hot sun. Yet each row of wind rippled dunes was a barrier between them and Thumb's Apaches. At the crest of each dune Shelter stood panting, searching the range behind them. There was no sign of the Chiricahua.

But then there never was until it was too late.

The gray was beat. Shell took the gold and shouldered it, the weight of it thrusting him deeper into the endless dunes. Drusilla walked beside him, eyes unfocused, falling and rising to struggle onward.

"How much more? There can't be much more," she gasped as Shell gave her a swallow of the warm water from the canteen, dampening the gray's mouth with his scarf soaked in water from the waterbag.

"No. It's not much farther," Shell answered. His tongue was like a stick in his mouth, his throat dry, gravelly, the backs of his hands were burned to masses of blisters.

The end of the field of dunes was in sight, in fact. They gradually flattened and were swept away by the winds. But beyond them was only more desert. As far as the eye could see, stretches of bare earth broken intermittently by low, cactus studded hills and jagged washes cut by winter floods.

Drusilla looked up, toward the barren, seemingly limitless desert beyond the dunes and tears filled her eyes, tears dried rapidly by the arid atmosphere. She made a helpless gesture.

"How . . . ?"

"I don't know how, but we will make it." Shell squinted into the sun, trying desperately to make something out. Anything he might recognize from the intensive, detailed descriptions Abe Turpin had given him in Leadville. Yet none of it resembled the flat maps Turpin had sketched.

He knew only that they had to get out of the dunes, and begin moving westward once more, toward the far mountains. How long could they walk without water, with the horse faltering?

Shelter had no idea, but he had already made one decision—if it came down to it, the gold would have to be abandoned. He would have traded it all for a gallon of clear, cool water right now; he did not mean to die for it.

Food was a consideration now that they were away from the train, although their dehydrated bodies did not crave food, still they would not make it far without something to eat, and Shell knew it.

He knew something about scavenging food on the desert from Turpin, but would it be enough?

Shell kept his eyes open for possible food sources, more to keep his mind busy than to satisfy a craving for it... the hours in the sun had fogged his mind. He found himself fumbling with basic decisions—who should ride, for how long, was it time for a sip of water? The day passed in a blur of heat. Colorless, soundless, empty, the desert seemed to have absorbed them, to have cleansed them of color, form, thought... they stumbled on.

When they could go no farther, they made their camp at the base of one of those wind-formed knolls which sprouted from the gray earth.

There was some nopal cactus growing thirty feet up along the formation and Shell clambered up, cutting a bushel full of the flat ears from the cactus. With the needles scorched off they would be forage for the gray, supplying it with extra water from the pulp, some nutrition.

Drusilla sat where she had fallen, against the knoll, in the shade where the heat was still intense. Sundown was an hour off.

She watched morosely as Shell started a small fire, using dry cactus for fuel and scorched the spines of the nopal.

"What's that for?" she asked.

"The horse."

She nodded and said nothing else, watching as if hypnotized as Shell turned the flat cactus on a stick, burning them.

"Do you want a little water?" Shell asked. Drusilla nodded and he sat beside her, holding the canteen to her badly chapped lips.

She drank, a trickle of water running down her throat, but said nothing else. Shell could hardly blame her. He was every bit as exhausted and if tomorrow did not bring a new source of water, a place where they had a reasonable chance of finding the security they needed to rest, it looked dim for their chances . . . almighty dim.

It was all most curious. Seven Fox sat his

pony atop a low ridge, studying the desert, the coming dusk. From where he sat he could see a wide sweep of land from the dunes where they had defeated the white intruders, the playa beyond. Nearly to the mountains. It was all curious.

A man on a single horse rode the desert, his squaw with him. Their horse was weighted down very heavily. What did it carry? Something of significance, for behind this white and his squaw was another rider.

And behind that man, still another lone rider. This one had a pack horse and much water. He too trailed the man with the squaw, Seven Fox believed.

And behind them all . . . a large band of whites, all armed, following the others so closely they could have used their tracks.

Seven Fox rolled it over in his mind slowly. Surely these whites did not pursue the woman—they had many in their towns; Seven Fox had seen them.

Then it was the man, or that which he carried. Since no man carries that which he does not need onto the desert, it was something valuable.

And quite heavy.

With the white man that meant only gold. It was not only the white man who knew how to use gold, however; fine weapons could be purchased with gold, much ammunition, desperately needed ponies to carry on the holy war.

Thumb must be told.

It seemed that many whites had chosen this

time to ride the desert. But there would not be enough of them. There were only enough to feed the coyote and the vulture.

Seven Fox turned his pony sharply and kneed it toward Thumb's camp, two miles distant.

11.

"Wake up!"

The man hovered over Drusilla Bentley and she blinked away the sleep in her eyes, recognizing Shelter Morgan by the dim light of the fading moon. It was bitterly cold dressed as she was, with no blanket but Morgan's coat.

"What is it?" She looked around, fright in her eyes.

"It's time to ride."

"It's the middle of the night," she objected as

he helped her to her feet.

"Two hours to sunrise. I figure to get a jump on the sun today—it's the only way."

"I don't think I can move," Drusilla said miserably. "I'm stiff—wobbly."

"I feel half dead myself, but we've got to ride, Dru, it's the only way."

She nodded placidly and walked to the saddled gray horse, surprised to find frost underfoot. Shell steadied the horse as she swung a long leg up across the saddle and Shell smiled as he caught a view of a tiny ridge of pink through the dark bush between her legs.

"What's funny?" Drusilla wanted to know.

"I just admire the way you get up on a horse," he answered.

"You . . ." she smiled. "I thought you were half dead!"

"Half. Ain't that half, I guess," he said, tugging his hat down. He turned then, leading the gray across the rocky, moon frosted desert toward those far mountains.

They made good time in the cool hours before dawn, following the sinking moon which had flattened, gone to a pale bluish hue as the horizon swallowed it up.

At the first flash of the golden sun, the desert seemed to change, taking on its terrifying aspect once more, becoming the enemy.

A long line of pure gold edged the eastern horizon, crowning the Gallinas.

Long shadows crept from beneath the rocks, pointing the way to the western mountains. The fragile morning dew evaporated within half an hour after sunrise, and the desert again became a searing hell.

"Hold up," Shell said.

Drusilla sat on the gray, watching as Shell walked to a quartet of Spanish dagger—yuccas growing against the face of a low knoll. They were flowering. Clusters of pale yellow blossoms clung to the upper reaches of the desert plant.

Shell collected as many as possible and brought them back in his saddlebags. He tasted one, frowned and popped the whole blossom into his mouth, chewing it slowly.

"That is good to eat?" Drusilla asked in amazement.

"I wouldn't say it was good," Shell shrugged. "But it's to eat."

Drusilla took a handful of the blossoms and tried one. "Bitter. There can't be much in them to keep us alive."

"It's something," was all Shell could say. "Turpin said the Indians eat 'em. There's not much else to offer," he added, looking across the barren land.

"No." Drusilla munched another blossom, and another. It was something.

There was no sign of game, and Shell was reluctant to fire a weapon had there been any. Using knowledge he had gained only second hand, they scavenged whatever they found—the beans of the thorny mesquite which the gray seemed to favor, the leaves of the low-growing agave which Shell meant to boil later, and which

Turpin said the Indians also used for making soap.

It was stringy, bitter fare, all of it, but it filled their stomachs—undoubtedly the Indians had methods of making it all into something more palatable, but Shell knew none of them.

The moisture from the plants helped some, and it also gave Drusilla something to be alert for—she seemed to have grown fond of the yucca blossoms.

They rested through the heat of the day, beneath a jerry-rigged canopy: Shell stretched his saddle blanket above the ground with four twigs driven into the sand. It was not much, but at least they were able to keep their heads out of the sun. Drusilla even managed to nap.

Shell watched her as she slept. A beautiful dark eyed woman, with raven black hair to her shoulders. Her chemise showed those magnificent breasts, the large, dollar-sized aureolas, dark brown beneath the white of the gown, the enticing nipples . . . but what sort of woman was she? Who, in fact was she? What went on in that mind?

They were camped next to a jumble of white, broken rocks for the extra shade it provided in close, and Shell restlessly sat up, studying the mound which was no more than thirty feet high, fifty across. Nothing grew there, nothing moved.

Then, unexpectedly, he found himself looking into a tiny set of eyes and he froze.

It was a chuckawalla staring back. Shell knew nothing about this ugly, overgrowed cousin of the lizard but that it would swell up in that crevice if frightened, and even a cougar couldn't pull it loose. That and the fact that a chucka-walla was fine eating. Turpin swore he had eaten them.

This one looked to have three pounds of meat on him, maybe, and that was more meat than Shell had seen in four days.

But how to get him out? Shell decided to try it quickly before the chuckawalla, which already looked uneasy, backed deeper into the crevice. Those tiny black eyes glittered out of its green, leathery skull as it watched Shell . . . maybe the first stand-up animal the chucky had ever seen.

Without moving his head, Shell slid his hand over and pulled one of his stakes from the ground. The blanket sagged onto Drusilla, she did not awaken or make a sound.

Slowly, with the chuckawalla's eyes watching intently, Shell fished for his bowie and began sharpening the end of the stake. The idea was to kill the chucky with one quick thrust before its natural defensive mechanism could be triggered. There would be only one chance.

Shell had the stake sharpened now and he got carefully to his knees, every movement slow, every movement scrutinized by the wary reptile.

The chucky flinched, its head drawing back on its leathery neck as Shell slowly hefted the short spear, and Shell froze, holding his breath. He could see gaps between the big lizard's sides and the walls of the crevice when it breathed, so it hadn't inflated yet—not just yet.

He wanted to get a hair closer, but dared not. It had to be one blow and only one to do the job. The brain or the heart . . . just where the hell was a lizard's heart anyway?

Shell concentrated on a point between the chucky's glittering eyes, holding steady. Then he jabbed, with all of his strength.

The chuckawalla leaped, squirmed, twitched. But it was dead. Shell quickly thrust his hand into the crevice and grasped the chucky, which was all of three feet long pulling it from its den.

Shell grinned, turning it over with satisfaction, examining the leathery hide, the fat haunches and tail. Drusilla still slept and he let her, butchering the chucky.

He started a tiny fire and cut the chucky into strips. Fine-grained, white meat, Turpin said it tasted like chicken, as many reptiles do. Shell felt the saliva building in his mouth as he watched the flesh broil.

He burned his fingers taking a strip from the fire, juggled it and blew on it, then tasted it. With immense satisfaction he scooted to where Drusilla lay and he touched her shoulder.

She sat upright immediately, blinking with confusion.

"Dinner's served," he announced, handing her the strip of meat. She took it, examining it curiously. She glanced toward the gray as if to assure herself Shell had not butchered the horse, then daintily tasted it.

"Delicious," she judged. Greedily she ate it, licking her fingers. "Is there more?"

155

"About two pounds. All you want now. We'll carry the rest for tonight."

"I can't believe it. I've never eaten anything . . . what is it, Shell?"

"You might not want to know."

"Sure I do," she insisted.

"Well," he grinned, "it comes packaged in green skin when it's alive . . ."

"Never mind! You're right—I don't want to know, I only want more."

They each ate a half a pound or so of the chucky, washed down with sparing sips of water, and it left them revived, feeling stronger, more optimistic. The Peloncillos Mountains loomed larger with each hour they traveled, and now for the first time in a while, Shell felt they just might make it.

The terrain was different now, sloping uphill toward the dark foothills in the distance. There were giant saguaro cactuses, arms stretching skyward, and enormous barrel cactus where Shell was able to find damp pulp for the horse, saving water for them—enough to stretch that little they still carried.

Spanish dagger dominated the rocky slopes, with here and there a mesquite bush and once a lonesome, barren ironwood tree—so hard the wood had to be harvested with sledge hammers, not axes.

They made camp on a low rise, not five miles from the first of the Peloncillos foothills, and blessedly, even the wind had cooled. The long shadows of the mountains brought them an early dusk and they sat chewing the remainder of the chuckawalla meat, supplemented with mesquite beans and yucca blossoms, drinking a full cup of water each.

"So little . . ." Drusilla was meditative. "It takes so little to make life endurable. And yet we ravage and kill. Fight over the useless, the unnecessary. Why?"

"You're asking me?" Shell was no shakes as a philosopher, but he mulled it and said, "I reckon it's because most of us don't know how easy life is until we're in a situation like this one. A full stomach, a shelter, a friend or two . . . that should be enough."

"You left out something," Drusilla said coyly. They sat next to one another on the ground, and she clenched his arm now, leaning her head against his shoulder.

"A little lovin' don't hurt," Shell allowed. He tilted her mouth up and kissed her, gently, for both of them had blistered lips.

"And a lot?" Drusilla asked, her dark eyes searching his.

"A lot don't hurt neither," Shelter Morgan said. He lay her gently back and she waited, watching as his fingers unbuttoned her gown.

He started at her throat, peeling the gown away as he uncovered her, his lips going to those breasts, her abdomen, her thighs in turn. Her arms stretched out to him in the twilight and he threw his shirt aside, dropping his jeans.

She wasted no time on this night. As Shell's body met hers her fingers went between his legs, grabbing for his cock. Frantically she worked to position it, holding it just at the entrance for a long minute, moving it in slow circles.

Shell's hand went to her crotch, found Drusilla's and their fingers intertwined, working together as they slowly guided him into her hot depths.

Their fingers were coated with Drusilla's juices, and they dipped into her even as Shell's shaft slammed home. Drusilla began panting, nibbling at Shell's ear as she guided his fingers to her clitoris.

There was enough work for the both of them to do. Touching, searching. As Shell's fingers traced a pattern against Drusilla, her hand found Shell's erection and she held him halfway in, her fingers stroking the other half excitely.

Abruptly she stopped and Shell slid his hand away too. He wanted to rock against her, to slam it to her and that was the way she wanted it now, hard and fast. She clenched his hard buttocks, pulling him home.

He bit at her throat, her nipples and she panted.

"Harder. Tear me apart. I need it."

She was bucking like a mustang mare now, her pelvis slamming again and again against his, her fingers clawing at his hips.

"I want you to . . ." her voice broke into a moan, and her hips thrashed from side to side. She panted, lifting her hips, and tore at his back. "You . . ." she could not find the words. Instead a slow, rolling growl of satisfaction came to her lips and Shell felt her come undone. Quivering, relaxing. Quivering again as she tensed under him.

Her thighs were wet with it now and her heart raced wildly next to Shell's as he stiffened and began a slow, deep thrusting which brought Drusilla back. Again she began, her renewed motion less vigorous, slower, with a deeper feeling.

"Shell . . ." she barely breathed it as she came again, and Shelter filled her with his own torrential climax. They lay still in the night, lightly touching, saying nothing as night closed in around them.

Shelter awoke with a start. He had not meant to fall asleep, but he had. Drusilla, still beneath him, slept deeply. He slipped from her and she murmured in her sleep, her hand twitching toward him. But she slept.

Shell sat up, pulled his shirt on and stood, studying the backtrail.

And still they came. There in the distance, by the faint light of the rising moon he saw the twist of rising smoke, white against the black desert.

The night was growing chill and he covered Drusilla with his jacket. Then, with his Winchester propped beside him, Shell watched the desert, asking questions to which he found no answers.

They did not start until dawn the following morning. The land was rugged, broken, ascending, and it required full light.

There was no trail upward, just a series of

game trails and water cut chutes. The gray had to work to scramble up many of the inclines, and it was a long way up and over the mountains, yet Shell felt confident, strong.

He had started recognizing the landmarks Turpin had given him, and he knew that once on the mountain it would be difficult for Thumb to run them down. Shell was mountain born, mountain bred, and although these dry, lifeless creations of nature were far different from the pine clad hills he had roamed as a boy, still the land tilted and fell, and that was enough to make him feel nearly at home after the flat, trackless wasteland beyond.

He had it in mind to stick to the mountains, if possible, rather than descending again to the desert. With luck they would be able to follow the range to within twenty miles of Fort Bowie, and with every mile they closed the Chiricahua would be less likely to hit them.

Thumb, demented warrior he was reputed to be, must even respect the guns of the cavalry. Which again made Shelter wonder about the smoke . . .

Was it possible they had just happened to get ahead of a troop movement? Who else would feel so confident of their strength that they proudly burned huge campfires in the heart of Thumb's desert?

They came up a long gorge, and now here and there Shell spotted timber. Some growing along the ridge lines where great layers of ancient rock had been thrust up by faulting, by prehistoric earthquakes.

The land had been upthrust, folded, shifted and slammed to level. Everywhere the mountains showed the marks of primitive chaos. Ridges folded like badly shuffled cards.

Drusilla was fascinated as well, her head was constantly turning, studying the work of a mad nature. Yet there was a raw beauty to it, and here and there pockets of wildflowers: Windmills, elegant in their magenta hues, pretty, delicate yellow Limoncillos.

A healthy stand of cedar clustered on a narrow ledge not more than an acre wide, showing good water higher up. Shell meant to move up, and they climbed toward the timber.

The wind was actually chilly now. Shell guessed they were at five thousand feet or so. The desert all around them appeared as a bluish white sea.

They rode a narrow ribbon of a trail along the eastern slope. Now that trail branched, the right fork running toward the summit and toward the west where they needed to get.

Yet Shell recognized the trail now, the horse-head shaped peak, and he recalled Turpin having told him that the track petered out above at a sheer cliff, and he headed to the left—a road which was supposed to wind a ways south and then double back, taking a meadow pass through the mountain range.

He thought now of Abe Turpin, gratefully. He owed that old desert rat plenty, and if he got out of this alive he meant to look up Turp and buy him the biggest meal money could buy—and the way Turp could eat, that wouldn't be cheap.

From time to time, while resting the gray, Shell gazed out across the desert, but he saw no pursuit. Of course, they were high above the flats now, and the wind which groaned in the canyons up above also was stirring up sand and dust on the desert.

"The Apaches?" Drusilla asked, slipping up beside him.

"I don't see anything," he said. "Maybe we've beat the odds."

Still he worried. No doubt Thumb's people knew many ways through the mountains. Yet, as he told Drusilla, "It can't be seventy miles to Bowie, maybe much less."

"Then you've done it," Drusilla said. He tried to shrug it off, but she insisted. "You promised you'd take care of me. See me through. You lived up to it, Shelter. I'll never be able to thank you."

"You just have." He took her by the shoulders and kissed her forehead, finding it cool beneath his lips. "And several times . . . back there."

"You gave me just as much," Drusilla said. Little embarrassed Shelter Morgan, but folks thanking him for what he had done did embarrass him. After all—what else could he have done?

"Let's find a camp," he said, turning away, leading the gray up the trail which now neared the high meadows, Drusilla trudging after him, her arms folded across her breasts, a slight smile playing on her full lips.

12.

The high trail, true to Turpin's description, wound southward through narrow valleys, small meadows where water was available if not plentiful, where there was graze for the horse.

For two days they followed the trail south, and on the second day Shell shot a deer which they gorged themselves on. The cool air, fresh meat and water had returned their strength. Shell felt as fresh as ever, but for a nagging pain here and there, a raw burn on his neck and hands.

It was three hours after sunrise on the third day. They rode through scattered pine and oak, paralleling a tiny, winding creek. They came up toward a notch in the gray granite hills, and Shell saw it.

Unbelieving, he rode forward another fifty feet, Drusilla, riding behind him, apparently had not noticed. The wind gusted up through the notch, a dry wind off the desert below. Shell took off his hat and wiped his brow, letting the wind riffle through his shaggy blond hair.

"Get down," he told Drusilla, and she did so. Then Shell stepped out of the saddle and walking a few steps with her, he lifted a pointing finger. "Look."

Drusilla could see nothing but a brown splotch against the vast whiteness. She shaded her eyes.

"What is it?"

"What is it?" Shell repeated. "Woman, that is Fort Bowie!"

"Fort . . . we're through? We've made it!"

She turned wide, incredulous eyes to Shell.

"Not exactly," Shell said slowly, "but I'm damned if I can think of any way we shouldn't make it now."

"Shell!" She threw her arms around him, knocking his hat off. "You did it. Just as you promised."

She kissed his mouth, clung to him and stepped back, and then she said, "I've got to pay you for this."

"Later," he shrugged.

"No," she insisted, smiling. "Now."

164

Drusilla went to the gray, slipping the heavy canvas sack from behind the saddle. Deftly she untied the sack while Shell watched, hands on hips.

"I can't take any of that gold," Shell objected.

"No?" Drusilla smiled across her shoulder. "Then how about *this*?"

She turned and stood, still smiling sweetly. In her hand was a chrome derringer.

"You're kidding."

"Not a bit. Unbuckle your gunbelt, Shell. This isn't much of a gun, I know. But at this range a child couldn't miss."

Carefully Shell did as he was told. Few things scared him more than a woman with a gun. "You mind tellin' me what this is, Dru? You think I'm going to rob you, is that it?"

"Toss that gunbelt as far as you can," she said, nodding her head. Shell did as he was told.

"I don't get this," he told her.

"No?" Drusilla shook her head, not believing him. "You should. Earl put this pistol in the bag, Shell. My brother was a very thorough man."

Shell cocked his head, waiting for her to go on. All the time he was watching the sun glint on that chrome derringer.

"Earl did some asking around about you," Drusilla continued.

"And what did he find out?"

"What do you think? That you worked for Butterfield!"

"I worked . . ." Shell laughed. "That was only for two days. Anyway, what does that matter?"

"You're joking! Whose gold do you think that is, Shell? Butterfield gold, of course. Taken in those stage hold-ups.

"Earl and I were with them, you see. Don't look surprised—I'm very good with a gun, Shell."

"But you got greedy," Shell suggested.

"I wish you wouldn't put it like that." Drusilla swept back her hair with one hand. "We simply had enough. Earl thought things were getting too hot, so we packed out one night, meaning to get to Mexico."

"I guess Thumb put a monkey wrench in that plan."

"That's right. So we joined the Quaker wagon train. Hoping that such a large party would frighten the Apaches off . . . of course that didn't work."

"No." Shell shook his head. "But I'm not after that gold, Dru. I never was. I rode shotgun for Butterfield to pay my passage to Pueblo, that's all."

"Don't give me that!" she snapped. "You poked around. You found the gold. You asked questions about Virgil Plum."

"What's Plum got to do with this?" Shell asked.

No sooner had he asked that then he caught the shadows weaving through the timber beyond the meadow. Drusilla still watched Shell, her derringer levelled on him, so she was aware of nothing but the slowly changing expression on Shelter Morgan's face, an expression she could not fathom until she glanced across her shoulder and saw them as well.

Twenty horses moved down onto the meadow. They were spread widely out, and each carried a heavily armed man. Their leader . . . Shell had heard the old adage about speaking of the devil, but never seen it work like this. . .

It was Virgil Plum.

Slowly they rode, and now Shell could see the expression on Plum's face alter. He had been smirking triumphantly before, but now as he searched for and found Shell's identity in his mind, the smirk broadened to a vicious grin. He heeled his horse ahead.

Drusilla turned, trembling. She lowered the derringer futily. Plum reined in, a shower of dust sifting over them and he swung down, walking to Drusilla. With a clenched fist he backhanded her across the mouth, slamming her to the earth, wrenching the pistol from her hand.

"You little two-timing bitch," Plum panted. "Thought you'd make Mexico did you? Where's the gold?"

Meekly Drusilla lifted her hand, pointing out the sack. Blood trickled from her torn mouth. Deliberately Plum picked up the sack and counted it roughly.

"Seems to all be here," he said to a second, trail-dusty man with a long jaw and a growth of beard.

As he spoke, however, Plum's eyes remained on Shell, glittering with evil pleasure. He handed the sack to the other man and walked forward, spurs clinking to where Shelter Morgan stood waiting.

"Howdy, Plum," Shell said.

"I don't believe it!" Plum threw his head back and laughed. He was dirty, his eyes red-rimmed, his shirt torn. He smelled of salt, sweat and tobacco. "Look, boys. Look at this man here," he said loudly. "This here's a man come two thousand miles to die."

"Why deny it to him?" the second man said. He held the bag of gold now. Lanky, scarred, he had his hand on his pistol butt.

"Oh, I won't," Plum said, enjoying himself thoroughly. "Morgan—you beat all. How'd you get tied up with this thievin' slut?"

"We're both Quakers," Shell said, and Plum's fist slammed into Shell's jaw, spinning his head around. He could taste the blood and he stood glaring at Plum. "Don't you ever get enough gold, Plum?"

"No. Not as long as there's more out there," the big man replied.

"I'd watch myself, were I you," Shell said to the scar-faced man. "I've seen how Plum takes his cut of gold."

Plum's face turned crimson and he moved in again, throwing a knee to Shell's groin, and as he doubled up with the pain, Plum threw a savage uppercut, catching Shell on the point of the chin. He went down and sat there, blood streaming from his nose.

"Want me to shoot him?" scarface said. The man seemed almighty anxious to use that big Colt.

168

"No."

"We can't drag him. . ."

"Shut up, Shields! I've got my reasons," Plum shouted. He stood, fists clenched, over Shell, mouth open with his heavy breathing for a minute before he spun back toward Drusilla who sat crumpled against the earth still.

"You. You and your damned brother! Well . . . Earl got his, and I wish you'd of got it in the same way." He gloated, watching her face pale as he went on. "Yes, Earl's good and dead. But it wasn't us—it was done right. The Apaches got him."

"Don't . . ." Drusilla covered her face, but Plum slapped her hands away.

"I'll tell you how it was." Plum crouched beside her, eyes bright, enjoying her torment. "We found him three days back. Only it didn't look much like your fancy brother, not like the dude, Earl Bentley. Know why?"

"I don't want to know," Drusilla moaned.

"Girlie," Plum went on. "I've had a long hard ride after you—that desert's hell! Hell! And I've been savoring this, wanting to tell you what your fancy brother looked like when I found him."

"Leave her alone, Plum," Shell said, but Plum didn't even glance his way. The outlaws sat on their horses, grinning. A few had stepped down to get the kinks out.

"He was staked to the ground, Dru. Looked kind of funny," Plum had tipped his hat back. He scratched his whiskered throat. "Looked kind of funny, didn't he, Shields?"

"Naw." The lanky man shrugged. "Except for havin' his nose cut off, he didn't look bad."

The outlaws laughed and Shell felt his gut tighten. Plum was far from through. He scooted nearer to Drusilla, breathing into her face as he said. "His nose was trimmed off. Neat as pie."

"And his ears." Shields reminded him.

"Yeah—the Apaches took them ears too. Outside of that . . . oh, and he didn't have no hair to speak of."

Drusilla had begun sobbing. Wretching, convulsive sobs which wracked her body. Plum had no mercy in his black heart, however, and he kept it up.

"Tell you the truth, Earl looked kinda pale. I figure Thumb wanted to know where the gold was. Wanted to know real bad . . . way they kept at him.

"You see, girlie, after they snipped off his nose and his ears, they started in to some serious work. Earl was staked down and his belly ripped open while he was still alive. Then they heated up some rocks and put inside of his living guts. And I swear—I wish they'd got both of you too!" Plum was drunk with his own venom. He squatted near Drusilla a long while, watching her sob.

Abruptly he stood and walked back to Shelter Morgan. "The time comes, Morgan—I've learned a few things from them Chiricahua."

At that Plum's boot swung out and he caught Shell flush on the jaw, sending him sprawling. Shell tried to get up, clawing at the dirt, but

Plum stomped down on his fingers, grinding them to bloody pulp.

"Let's go," Plum said abruptly. "Them Apaches are still back there."

Someone dragged Shell to his feet. Roughly they shoved him toward the gray, threw him onto the saddle and tied him there, his hands lashed tightly to the pommel. Drusilla was thrown on behind him and a rope was thrown over both of them.

They rode slowly out, Shell's head still reeling from the beating. Plum led the way southward, toward Fort Bowie. His spread was somewhere near here, and it would be there Shell and Drusilla were being taken—though why Plum had not killed him outright, Shelter could not figure.

It was the one thing he did not understand—the rest had come clear. Drusilla and Earl had been with Plum's gang, riding out of their Arizona Territory stronghold to raid the goldfields of Colorado, then retreating again to their border hideout. Perhaps Plum had chosen this area only because Mexico was a stone's throw away.

At any rate, it explained why Plum disliked visitors, was regarded as a loner in the Fort Bowie area.

Drusilla and Earl had taken their chance and lost. Thumb had a deal to do with that—undoubtedly their original escape plan had called for a quick traverse of the desert area, safe refuge somewhere in Mexico. But they hadn't made it, and vengeance among the outlaw gangs was swift and harsh.

It had been Plum's smoke Shell had seen since Pueblo, not Sheriff Teerlinck's. Teerlinck was probably busy getting himself re-elected right now on the strength of having run the outlaws out of Colorado.

It was all clear now. Shell had found the Butterfield bandits as well as the man who had helped butcher his soldiers away back in Georgia on that bloody afternoon.

He had found them—and now they would kill Shelter Morgan as well.

13.

The ranch was located on a low hill within sight of Fort Bowie itself. The brush around the house had not been cleared off, and so the sumac, sage and manzanita which proliferated in the area screened the spreading adobe house off until they were nearly on top of it. It was difficult for anyone to move through that tangle of chapparal without being seen and heard, and from what Shell could see there was only one way up—hardly a trail, the bed of a gravel-strewn gulley wound past several low hills.

On each of those hills a man with a Winchester was posted. They watched as the returning band of outlaws led their captives up onto the hill where the tile-roofed adobe sat.

It bothered Shell in a way—Virgil Plum was tough, mean. Yet he hardly seemed the type to have planned a layout like this or to mastermind a large, well-organized gang of outlaws.

The adobe had a long veranda in front, facing the north, with pole uprights bracing the roof. Long strings of red chili peppers hung drying from them. A few huge ceramic *ollas*—Mexican pots—with bright decorations lined the plank window sills; a man in a white shirt, wearing a pistol appeared in the doorway, watching them ride into the yard, and Shell knew his hunch was right.

He recognized the man, knew him immediately for the outlaw kingpin.

Of medium height, with receding dark hair, a hooked nose, he had no right arm. Shell knew him, knew him well. His name was Howard Twyner, out of Georgia.

It had been Major Twyner, and he had been Plum's commanding officer. Now the murderer had become Plum's warlord, the leader of this gang of hold-up artists.

Twyner's sour little expression hardly changed as Shell and Drusilla were dragged from the horses and shoved roughly up onto the porch.

"Look what I found!" Plum said triumphantly. He put a boot to Shell's back and shoved. Shelter slammed into the wall and slid down.

"How did it go?" Twyner asked as if Shell were the farthest thing from his mind, a detail to be attended to when he had the time.

"It's Shelter Morgan!" Plum said proudly. Twyner made a small, disinterested gesture and Plum shook his head. "It went all right," he answered.

"Her?" Twyner was looking at Drusilla, ragged, dirty, still dressed in her nightgown and Shell's buckskin jacket.

"Dru and Earl tried to cross us, Major. They made a run for it. They lost."

"That's disappointing, Drusilla," Twyner said, wiping the bridge of his nose with a forefinger. "So pretty to die for a few dollars." He sighed and shrugged, turning toward the door. His eyes fell finally on Shell.

"Captain Morgan . . . you took your time getting here," he said.

"I had a few other stops." Shell muttered.

"Yes—I'll bet you did. You'll have to tell me about it later. Lock him up, Virgil. The root cellar will do."

"Yes, Major." He took Shell's arm roughly. "Get up, Captain Morgan. We've a room for you," he said smiling mockingly.

Shell was dragged and pushed through the long hallway of Twyner's house. He did not fight it, but kept his eyes open, studying the layout of the house. They had passed first through a tile-floored entranceway, and through an open door, Shell had caught a glimpse of Twyner's den, or

175

office beyond—a huge, dark-wooded desk sat there, a pair of longhorns on the wall.

Off the corridor were a series of small rooms, all with the doors closed—probably guests' sleeping quarters. A second hallway intersected this corridor and it led to an isolated room which might be Twyner's bedroom.

The house was cool, dark, of adobe with plastered walls, great beams supporting the ceiling. Shell was halted then turned to the right, shoved into a white, open kitchen.

But just before they had taken that last turn he had seen her—a dark woman in a flowing red dress, a black lace mantilla across her shoulders, a high Spanish-style comb in her dark hair. Twyner's woman? It had to be, but she had looked at Shelter Morgan with sympathetic eyes . . .

"We're gonna borrow your root cellar, Rosa," Plum told the cook. A heavy, pocked woman, she shrugged, waving a wooden spoon. "Hope this suits you, Captain," Plum said, opening the massive door. "Course, if it doesn't, don't worry about it. You won't be stayin' long enough for it to make a difference." Plum scratched his head and grinned venomously. "You won't be stayin' nowhere much longer."

At that he shoved Shelter ahead and the heavy plank door was slammed shut behind him.

He stumbled forward into the darkness, falling heavily. There was a short flight of four rough stairs just at the doorway, and Shell had not seen them.

Slowly he got to his feet, brushing off. He looked around the room, his eyes slowly growing accustomed to the darkness. There was no light but the faint light through the iron grill in the door itself. No windows, no other doors.

It was a root cellar, warehouse, pantry. Shell searched the room, studying the earthern walls, the roof. It had been carved out of native earth, this cellar, and it was solid.

There were sacks of potatoes in the corner, tins of beef and fruit: peaches, apples on the shelves which had been set into the granite.

Lifting a barrel lid Shell found a gross of rough bars of lye soap. There was little else—salt sacks, twenty pounds of coffee.

Shell walked back up the steps to the door, peering out. Rosa, the cook, went about her business, humming to herself as she stirred a steaming pot. Beans, they were, by the smell.

"Hey!" Shell hissed. "Rosa!"

"No." She waved a hand without even looking.

"Rosa! I'm hungry. Those frijoles smell good."

She turned then, hands on her huge hips. She walked to the table in the center of the room and picked up a meat clever, showing it to Shell.

"You get this. *Silencio!*"

Shell turned and sank to the steps, removing his hat. His hand where Plum had taken a bootheel to it was raw, crusted with ugly scab, discolored, and his back was badly bruised. His jaw was tender as well, and probing around in his mouth, Shell found two loose teeth.

Well—they had told him it was bound to happen. Many folks in many places. They had warned him that he could only chase down the murderers until *they* caught him. And it appeared they had.

He could have let it lay—for that matter he could have taken his cut of the gold away back in Georgia and had himself a place like this, a herd of cows. Providing he wanted to grow a long beard. . .

He sure as hell would never have been able to look at himself in a shaving mirror again.

Shell sagged back and closed his eyes. His head ached and his stomach was raising Cain, but somehow he managed to sleep. It was a deep, untroubled sleep with only one dream he could remember . . . he was walking a high mountain pasture with a dark haired Indian girl on his arm . . .

The door slammed open and Shell leaped instantly to his feet, fist clenched, blinking into the light from the kitchen.

A man with a gun stood there, and he jabbed at Shell. "Back away."

A red-headed, stubby man Shell recognized from the trail, he did not have to speak twice. Shelter took two steps backward and the redhead turned.

"All right, Miss Alicia," he said.

Someone else was there, and she appeared now, silhouetted in the doorway. The Spanish girl—tall, elegant, her mouth was finely molded, without expression. She held a tray in her hands.

"The Major won't like this," Red said.

"Do be quiet, George," Alicia answered. "The girl was fed—we shall feed the man as well."

"It's a pure waste," George insisted, nodding at Shell. "He'll be dead come nightfall."

"Then this is entirely fitting," she said smoothly, setting the tray on the top step. "I understand it is customary for a condemned man to be served a last meal."

Red, he kind of shrugged and shook his head like he would never understand women and Alicia straightened up, her eyes fixed on Shell. And for a brief, fleeting moment he thought he read something akin to compassion in them.

"Enjoy it," she said. "It is little enough."

"Thank you, Ma'm, I . . ." Shell took a half step forward, but the woman was gone, George slamming the door, locking it behind her.

Shell stood meditatively a moment, wondering if he had read anything in those eyes, or if it was just a vague hope finding substance.

He walked to the tray and found a plate of beans, a thick steak and some tortillas. He had no heart for eating just now, but his stomach was begging for it, so he sat on the steps, the tray on his knees.

He grinned when he saw the big steak and nothing to cut it with. There was neither knife nor fork, but it didn't slow him much. Shell scooped the beans up with the warm tortillas and gnawed the steak to the bone.

When he was through he felt better than he had a right to. They had fed him, penned him, and now they would be ready to butcher him.

It would not be long in coming, either. Looking through the grate in the door, he could see daylight fading through the kitchen window. He looked again at those bars set into the solid oak of the door grate, and again he braced himself, testing the bars.

He pulled until his shoulders ached, until the perspiration trickled down his forehead, but there was no give to the grate. Who ever built that door had done it right—perhaps it had been intended all along to serve as a part-time calaboose.

Angrily Shelter slammed the palm of his hand against the door. It was hopeless and he knew it, yet he had been in tight spots before—there was no way he would give it up.

Yet all along he was thinking that escaping the root cellar would accomplish little. He would still have to get past twenty armed men and find some way of escaping them across the desert . . . very long odds indeed.

He sagged to the steps and watched as the light faded. When day was nearly done the door slammed open and there they stood, guns in hand.

"It's time, Morgan."

14

George was there—the red-headed outlaw, and the man who was so eager with a gun, Shields. Two other men Shell had seen stood back a way, shotguns in their hands.

"Think you got enough artillery?" Shell asked wryly.

"Step on out of there, Morgan," Shields said. There was a nasty inflection in his words. This was a man who killed and enjoyed it.

Shell came out of the root cellar, putting his

hat on, and they led him down the long corridor, to the front of the house. Twyner's door was closed and George stepped to it, rapping twice.

Outside Shell could see sundown edging the ragged clouds with crimson fire, the sky paling to a faint orange. The mountains were dark, distant. Doves winged homeward against the evening skies.

"Go on in," George said, gesturing with his six-gun. Shell stepped through the doorway, followed by George and Shields.

"Well . . ." Twyner looked up from his desk. He had on reading glasses and he unhooked them from his nose, standing to study Shell.

"You've made a long chase of it, Captain Morgan."

"I guess," Shell conceded. "I had three good reasons."

"Three?" Twyner's eyebrows knit with vague curiosity. From the corner Plum watched with an acid smile. Alicia stood near the window, her back to them, watching sundown fade the land.

"Three." Shell counted on his fingers. "Welton Williams, Dinkum, and Jeb Thornton."

"Them?" Twyner shrugged as if it were of no importance. "A lot of men died in that war, Morgan—you would have done better to forget it."

"They didn't die in the war, Major. They would have made it back to their homes, if it hadn't been for your greed."

"Greed?" Twyner seemed taken aback by that term. "It was simply building for our future—all

182

of us felt that way. The South was dead, ravaged, burned . . . what did we have for our service? Who would pay me what this was worth?" He held up the stump of an arm, waving it.

"No, Morgan, you are an idealist. You could have been well set up. We would have shared."

"I doubt that," Morgan said. "Recallin' how the offer was made."

"Well, nonetheless. You had your chance, you should have taken it. Money can buy a man's comfort." He waved a hand around. "I have everything. Land, home . . . Alicia. How could I own her without money."

The Spanish woman turned toward them, arms crossed beneath her shawl, and Shell saw a subdued fire in those coal black eyes which told him beyond a doubt that no matter what Twyner thought, he did not own that woman.

"The list," Plum said in a low voice.

"Oh, yes." Twyner unfolded a paper on his desk. "This was found in your roll, Morgan." He held up the list Shell had made. The list of every man who had participated in that massacre.

"You found your name," Shell said.

"Mine. Sergeant Plum's. You seem to have planned thoroughly." Twyner held the list up. "There are two names crossed out, I see. Gordon Wakefield, Leland Mason—you have settled up with them?"

"It was settled," Shell said, nodding slowly.

"Mason was a friend of mine," Twyner said.

"It figures."

"A good officer . . ."

"If you say so. He dressed well."

"Yes . . ." Twyner sagged to his chair. "I can only assume that your intention was to seek me out and assassinate me, Morgan. That will make it easier for me to order your death."

"I don't think you were having that much trouble anyway, were you?" Shell asked.

"No," Twyner admitted. "Very little."

Plum was grinning. He sat on the window sill, listening. Alicia had said nothing, would say nothing. Twyner had a hold on her, that was for sure. Besides, there was nothing to be said any longer, no way to wriggle out of this.

"I really don't know why Sergeant Plum bothered to bring you in, Morgan. Now someone will have to dig a grave, and the ground is hard this time of year."

He took the list, crumpled it up in his hand and tossed it to the floor, nodding to Plum at the same time. Red and Shields grabbed Shelter by the arms and turned him around, shoving him from the room.

It was cool on the porch, the diffused colors of sunset flooding the oaks beyond the ranch yard. Shell took it in, filling his lungs.

"Running out of guts, Morgan?" Shields asked coldly.

"It's a fine evening," Shell responded, his words soft, "I'm enjoying it."

"Take all the time you want," Plum said. "Take thirty seconds." Then he laughed, viciously and Shields joined him.

George was up on a horse, tossing a rope

across the low hanging limb of a massive oak tree. "It'd be simpler to put a bullet in his head," Shields commented.

"Major wants him hung," Plum answered, and that seemed to settle it. There was the sound of footsteps on the porch behind Shell and he turned his eyes to find Twyner there, Drusilla beside him.

"Dru?" She looked like hell. Her eyes were ringed with black, her face pale as a ghost's. Shell's eyes flashed. "You're not going to hang her too?"

"No." Twyner spared a grim smile. "I am a practical man, Captain Morgan. Drusilla has great value below the border—she will be sold. I only wanted her to understand what might happen if she should fail to cooperate again. You shall provide the lesson.

"Goodbye, Captain Morgan." Twyner snapped a quick, mocking salute and nodded to Plum who kicked Shell off of the porch, sending him sprawling in the dust.

"Game's up, Morgan. Crawl on over there."

Shell tried to get to his feet but Plum kicked him again. "I said crawl!"

Shelter Morgan's head was reeling. Blood trickled down from his nose. They stood around him, laughing, watching. A fury was building in him, the fury of desperation.

"Crawl!" Plum shouted. His boot toe arced toward Shell's head but Shell saw it coming and he grabbed Plum's boot, twisting hard. He heard the crack of bone as he continued to twist it,

185

throwing Plum aside as he came to his feet.

Plum was on his knees, frothing at the mouth. He drew back the hammer on his Colt and locked eyes with Shelter Morgan's cool blue eyes.

"You can shoot. Hang me—I'll crawl for no man," Shell said evenly. The blood raced through his temples, his heart pounded. They would kill him—well, let them.

But he'd be damned if he'd crawl for them!

"It's your choice," Plum said, raising that pistol.

"Sergeant!"

Plum glanced toward Twyner, his finger twitching on that cold steel trigger. "He'd rather be shot, Major."

"Damn what he wants, do as I say!" Twyner said with annoyance.

Plum tried to get to his feet, but he couldn't make it. Shell had broken or badly twisted his ankle. Plum sagged back to the earth, cursing profusely, vehemently.

"Come on," Shields said from beside Shell. "And don't try anything like that with me. I don't owe that Major Twyner a damned thing. I'll shoot you and smile."

They tied Shell's hands in the shadow of the swinging noose. He stood watching the subdued fire of the sunset sky. He saw an owl winging low across the chapparal. A horse blew somewhere. The wind was cool against his sweat-soaked shirt.

Drusilla stood arms at her side, her head a ghost's head, her eyes vacant, pain-filled. Alicia, beside her, turned a quarter away, placing her shawl over her head.

Red was mounted and he slipped behind Shell on his buckskin pony, the noose in his hands. Red lifted the noose, nodded and fell to the earth, blood streaming from a gaping hole in the side of his head.

Shell flinched. Red rolled at his feet, half his skull torn away. Then, seemingly seconds later the roaring sound of gunfire reached Shell's ears. He glanced toward Shields, whose gun was smoking as he dropped to a crouch, and for a split second Shell thought that Shields, for some unfathomable reason, had killed Red.

Then the bullets sang all around them. The ground at Shields' feet was torn up by slugs. Plum, hopping on one foot raced toward the porch, and guns from the house opened up as the first of the Apache ponies leaped into the yard.

A man screamed. A painted, naked brave rode past, bouncing to the earth as a bullet from the house tagged home.

Shell spun and raced toward the brush clotted ravine, seeing an Apache on foot veering toward the house, hearing another scream—this one a woman's as the roar of gunfire built to a deadly, incredible crescendo.

Shell's hands were still firmly bound behind him. He had no idea where he was running but into the brush. All he knew was that it was run or die—this seemed no time for false valor.

The sky was a crimson wash across the black land. The perimeter of the tangled chaparral thicket was within twenty yards now, and Shell ran without looking back, hearing the angry whine of bullets ricocheting, the pounding of horses hooves and an occasional cry of pain.

The brave loomed up suddenly in front of him.

He was bare to the waist, painted wildly with zig-zag lines across his face and chest. In his hands he held a Henry repeater and he shouldered it as Shell rushed toward him.

There was no way to escape, no way to fight, so Shell simply lowered his head and kept on coming. He hit the brave low in the chest as the Henry exploded across his shoulder, and they tumbled to the earth, the rifle falling free of the Apache's hand.

Shell was on his feet first and as the Chiricahua groped for his repeater, Shell swung a boot with all the strength he had, and the Indian sagged back, blood streaming from a badly split mouth.

Shell plunged into the brush, running low, hands tied behind him.

Darkness was covering them now, and the thick brush might—might hide him. If he got deep enough. The brush tore at his face and arms, thorns lashed his legs as he stumbled and ripped his way through the incredible tangle.

He ran for fifty feet, stumbled and slid for twenty more down a rocky, hidden ravine, then sat silently for a moment. He heard nothing behind him. There was still rifle fire from the yard, or near it.

Shell got slowly to his feet, moving through

the gathering shadows more deeply into the thicket. There was a pale half moon rising above the mountains, still the glow of sunset's last fiery moments to the west.

Shelter tried scaling a steep bank, but without the use of his hands it was impossible and he rolled down again, slamming his chin against a rock.

Was he far enough away? There was no way to be sure.

What he needed was to find a hiding place, to somehow work those strips of rawhide off his wrists.

He went up a small gulley, kicking a low barrel cactus in the darkness, the thorns piercing his boot, sending bitter pain through his foot.

Swallowing a curse, Shell went on. The brush was even thicker now, the woody manzanita knit upon itself, barring any progress. So he got to his belly and slithered.

The last moment of sundown flashed on a high streamer of cloud and was swallowed up. The twilight lingered briefly, and the pale moon gave a dull glow to the eastern sky.

Shell found himself in a tiny hollow, deep within the thicket, from the hair he found there, it belonged to a deer—or had. It was his for a time.

He sat still for a long half hour, listening, only listening. Could any man, white or red move through that thicket without making a sound—Shell did not think so.

Still he listened, watching the moon sketch

narrow shadows beneath the manzanita brush. He searched the perimeter of the clearing which was only ten feet across at the widest, searching for something he did not find.

Yet back a ways, beneath a frost-browned laurel leaf sumac, he saw it. A sharp edged chip of granite the size of his hand and he stretched for it, dragging it out with a boot toe.

By twisting around, groping, Shell was able to pick the rock up and turn it, sharp edge up. Slowly then he began the awkward, painful process of sawing through the rawhide strips.

His hand cramped up and the thongs cut his wrists as he stretched them, but eventually one broke free. And then the other.

Panting Shell brought his hands before him, rubbing them, frowning at the raw grooves cut into his wrists, the badly torn back of the right hand where Plum had stomped him.

Yet he felt whole now; his hands brought him a sort of freedom, the ability to fight, to do. He ran a hand along his boot, finding the broken cactus spine. He yanked it free, wincing at the pain, the flood of poisonous itching.

Then for just a moment Shelter Morgan lay flat on his back, breathing deeply, watching the coming night.

He was in it this time, and deep. Beyond the brush lay open desert, and afoot, without water or defense he had no chance of making Bowie.

What then? He did not know what had happened at the ranch. There had been gunfire, men killed on either side. Had the Apaches been driven off? If so Twyner would be searching for Shell.

Perhaps the Chiricahua had won, or they were surrounding the house, waiting until morning. In that case the Apache and not Twyner would kill him.

He was caught between two hostile forces, ringed by the naked desert. Unarmed, afoot. "You do get yourself into them, Shelter Morgan," he told himself.

There was no easy way out of this one, perhaps no way at all.

And it was no consolation knowing that his next move would have to be back toward the ranch house. Only there could he find a horse, water, guns—if the guns did not find him first.

The rising moon hung across the empty desert. Shell watched it, letting the hours pass. Still it was silent above him. A deadly silence. It was midnight, no earlier, when Shell rose and slipped down into the ravine, working his way toward the battlefield.

15.

It was dark, cold, still. Shell crept through the chapparal toward the ranch house above him. The huge oaks surrounding the house were smeared, black blisters against the sky, the very tips of the trees haloed with the gold of the coming moon.

He crouched at the edge of the yard, eyes flickering, every direction, his breath coming in tight, knotted gasps.

Nothing.

Nothing moved in the house or near it, nothing he could see. There were no lights, but he had expected none. If the Apache were about, they were well concealed. The night was as silent as if nothing had ever happened, as if nothing had ever lived there.

Shell slipped from the brush, moving catlike through the shadows. A massive oak screened out the moon momentarily as Shell crept forward. He stopped, his every sense alert.

Nothing. He took several quick steps forward and then stopped, abruptly. Red still lay there, a gory reminder. Shell slipped the six gun from the dead man's holster and looked around.

Pressed against the trunk of the oak he was nearly invisible, or so he hoped, but the remainder of the yard was light, moon glossed. Once he stepped out of the shadow of the oak, he would offer a clear target for anyone watching.

Yet he would have to cross the yard, make it to the stables if he were to find a horse . . . if horses there were. Shell stepped forward and to one side, his eyes on the house. Then he bumped into it and he froze, muscles tight.

It dangled there, swaying now from Shell's nudge. The moon splotched the dead features of Virgil Plum as he hung from the rope. Shell watched the macabre sight for a moment. Plum had been slashed with a knife, his eyes put out. Then the Apaches had hung him with the very noose Plum had intended for Shell.

Shell took a deep breath and inched forward. There was still no movement, no sound, no scent

193

on the breeze which stirred the oaks.

Taking one last long look around, Shelter dashed for the house, not knowing what to expect. He leaped the steps and was to the porch in one bound. He pressed against the adobe wall, heart pounding. Nothing . . . were the Apaches gone, then? Or only patient?

The front door, he noticed now, was open—unlikely if there was anyone inside. Cautiously he eased toward the door. He stood at it for a moment, deciding.

Then he crouched, kicked the door full open and rolled inside, coming to his feet ready, gun in his hand and cocked.

But the house was cold, silent, empty . . . but for Drusilla. She lay just inside the door, a maroon colored splotch across the front of her white gown.

Shell crouched beside her, already knowing she was dead. He put a palm to her cool forehead, muttering a silent oath. She had never deserved something like this. But she had taken the wrong turn and that had put her in the wrong place at the wrong time.

"I won't forget you soon," Shell whispered. He touched her dark hair which seemed still alive, vibrant. "So long, Dru."

Shell moved slowly through the house, keeping his back to the wall, his gun cocked. From the looks of things the place was deserted. That would seem to indicate the Apaches had driven Twyner off.

It was surprising that the Indians hadn't

torched the house or ransacked it. But perhaps Thumb's only concern was the gold. He would not waste time in burning the house simply to prove a point, nor would he want his braves weighted down with booty . . . that was all conjecture. For all Shell knew it was the other way around.

Perhaps Twyner had Thumb on the run. It could be fatal to assume the house was empty now, to assume that the empty grounds outside were in fact empty, or would remain so.

Shell was not an assuming man. He moved cautiously, but quickly, finding the door to Twyner's office which he slid slowly open.

Empty. Shelter crossed the darkened room, finding his gear still stowed in the corner. He buckled on his gunbelt, sticking Red's gun behind his belt for a spare. Then he hefted his Winchester and roll.

He did not wish to exit by the front door in case someone was watching, and so he slipped down the long corridor toward the kitchen where he knew there was a back door.

Rosa lay on the kitchen floor, meat cleaver in her hand, a dead Apache brave beside her in a pool of blood. Shell stepped around them and hesitated, studying the gap between the house and the flat roofed, brush-walled stable. It was about thirty yards, all level ground. It was moon bright—a regular shooting gallery.

He had still not convinced himself no one was around. Perhaps he had taken them by surprise with his first move toward the house. Now they would be alerted. Was there even a horse there? He had no way of knowing.

Shell opened the door with the barrel of his Winchester and made his run.

It seemed the longest run of his life. Shell ran low, crouched over, eyes darting to the shadows. The stable seemed incredibly distant but finally he hit the door with his shoulder, bursting in to find a saddled horse standing there. And a man with a gun.

"Drop that rifle, Morgan."

"Take it easy."

"I'm takin' it easy. Just drop that Winchester."

Shell put it down gingerly, straightening up to face the man across his gunsights. He was battered, dirty, and it was a moment in the darkness before Shell recognized him.

Earl Bentley! It was incredible, but there he stood. "You're supposed to be dead, Earl," Shell said.

"I feel most dead," Bentley replied. "But as you can see, I'm hanging on."

"Drusilla . . ."

"I know. I saw her." Earl sagged against the wall of the stable, but when Shell took a step forward he lifted the muzzle of his Colt. "Stay there."

"All right." Earl looked unstable, perhaps it was exhaustion, the shock of finding Drusilla, but he knew Earl was hell on wheels with a six shooter and he had no inclination to try him.

He asked Earl conversationally, "Mind tellin'

me why you're not dead?"

A shadow of a smile played on Earl Bentley's lips. "That's what they thought?"

"Plum said he found you, skinned by the Apaches."

"It wasn't me." Earl shook his head. "I saw him too ... he was badly mutilated. Horribly ... he could have looked like anybody. I guess Plum figured it had to be me. He knew of no one else on the desert. I know who it was—I recognized his guns."

"Anyone I knew?"

"I reckon you're the reason he died," Earl said. "He was a man with too much pride: that cowboy from Dos Picos, Christman."

Christman. That town tough had followed Shell so far, onto the desert to have his revenge! It was incredible, but true apparently, and it gave Shell cause to consider what happens to men who carry their grudges too long ... men like himself.

"You know we can't stay here," Shelter said.

"No. I'm riding." Earl agreed.

"And me?"

"I can't have a Butterfield man on my backtrail, Shelter. I'm sorry." There seemed to be genuine regret in Earl's voice, but he drew back that hammer anyway.

"I'm not a Butterfield man, Earl. It was Plum I wanted. Him and Twyner. From a long time back."

"You're the law?"

Shell shook his head. "No. Just a crazy man

like Christman. I've seen Plum hung, now I want the same for Twyner."

Earl rubbed his forehead with the back of his hand. He was unconvinced. "I can't believe you, Shelter."

"No? Think twice, Earl! I found that gold long back. Why keep travelling south? What would Donne have done if I told him I was Butterfield, if I showed him the gold! He would have drummed you out. Maybe turned the wagon train around, delivering you to Dos Picos.

"Anyway," Shell went on. "I reckon I had the chance to slip my gun on you a time or two out there. Like you did. We didn't. We rode with that uneasy truce between us. Hell, Earl—I don't want that damned gold. Let's ride together. You get what you want; I get Twyner. But let's be doing it soon, whichever it is. Both of them are getting farther away with every minute we jaw."

Earl's steady gaze met Shell's and he shook his head just slightly, making his decision. Slowly his thumb eased the hammer of his Colt down, and Shell breathed a sigh of relief.

"I don't know why, but I'm trusting you," Earl said.

"All right. Let's get with it then. There a saddle here?"

Earl nodded toward a saddle in the corner. Shell picked out a strapping chestnut pony and tied a lead rope on a black. "Better find you a spare horse too," he advised Earl. "We've some long riding ahead."

They were saddled and out of the stable in ten

minutes. The night was black, still. Shell looked around, "Which way do you guess?"

"I don't have to guess. Twyner's got another house below the border. A regular fortress, sitting up on a mountain. That's where he'd go. If he's still able."

If. If Thumb had the gold the game was up. He asked Earl, "Why do you figure Thumb pulled off? Darkness?"

"I don't think that makes a damned difference to this Apache. No," Earl said, "I think he jumped the gun, maybe didn't realize how many guns he'd find against him up here. I figure he pulled back to gather his braves. And I figure he'll be back, Shelter. He wants that gold—even worse than I do.

"But I was wanting it first," Earl said, and he was deadly earnest, "I mean to have it."

They rode southward, toward the border with the moon high in the sky. The desert spread out before them, weirdly glossed with yellow. The horses cast long, crooked shadows before them as they moved.

"We're maybe twenty miles from the border," Earl told Shell. "Morning should see us across. We won't be catching up with the Major, not unless Thumb caught him first."

Earl knew this country like the back of his hand, apparently. He had little trouble finding a concealed trail in a brushy ravine which cut through the dry hills, saving them miles.

There were no tracks Shell could make out across the desert but their own.

"Don't worry about that—this is my own little shortcut," Earl said. "He's heading south, all right."

An hour before sunrise they made camp in a wind-hollowed teacup of a cave where they could look out over the desert. They drank all the water they could hold and then boiled coffee, letting the horses graze in the dry but plentiful gramma grass.

"We'll make La Paloma first," Earl said over a cup of coffee. "Small town on the Mex side. They know me there. We'll eat, see what we can learn."

"You figure there's time to eat?" Shell asked.

"I figure we might as well, Morgan. Way I see it the Major's got enough lead on us to make that fortress of his. We'll have to climb that mountain and pluck him out—it'll be like robbing an eagle's nest, but there's no help for it. It's the only way."

Earl diagrammed the house as they rested, watching the hasty, golden sunrise, and from this sketch Shell could tell the house was just what Earl had termed it, a fortress. "If we had any sense, we'd give it up," he said quietly.

Earl Bentley did not answer. He had that gold fever and nothing short of a bullet would stop him.

If there were any way to work this without Earl, Shell would have pulled off, but there wasn't. He knew the territory, knew the house, the mountain it perched on.

But there was a lot Shelter didn't like about it.

As he had said, they rode with an uneasy truce between them. A fragile truce, it would take little to break it.

Once, tightening his cinch, he had looked up unexpectedly to find Earl Bentley's eyes on him, and the look they held was not that of a missionary. It was a wild, savage gleam. Not of hatred, but of a deeper, undefined emotion . . . perhaps approaching fear.

Whatever it was, Shell did not like it, and when they rode out Shell rode behind Earl Bentley, his Winchester across the saddle bows.

16.

La Paloma rested on a low, broken mesa six miles across the Mexican border. The town was squat, scattered, mostly of adobe with here and there a brush roofed hut, and one frame building, badly in need of paint—the cantina.

Shell tied up beside Earl and they dusted the alkali from their clothes before stepping up onto the weathered gray porch and walking into the dark, warm cantina.

"Señor Bentley!"

"Buenos tardes, Paco," Earl called to the man behind the bar. A balding, hugely mustached Mexican who wore his shirt sleeves rolled up, revealing massive, hairy forearms. *"Cerveza, por favor.* For me and *mi amigo!"*

Shell followed Earl to a table in the far corner. There were three or four men in the saloon. Two wore white peasant suits, the others were also Americans. None of them as much as glanced at Shell and Bentley.

Earl took off his hat, wiped back his hair and leaned back in a chair. Paco walked to the table and put two bottles of beer down. Wiping his hands on his apron the man glanced from Shell to Earl and back.

"A new man?" Paco asked.

"Friend of mine." Earl poured his beer, as did Shell. It was barely cool, but satisfying despite being some green. "Seen *El Mayor* Twyner today?"

"El Mayor? No. He is returned?" Paco asked.

"Quien sabe?" Earl shrugged, taking a deep drink. "Perhaps he is across the line? I've been away."

"No," Paco said, shaking his head heavily, "I have no seen him. *Me comunicaré contigo tan pronto le vea."*

"It doesn't matter," Earl said waving a hand. "I'll be seeing him soon anyway."

Shell sipped at his beer, watching as Paco walked away. Earl put his glass down and said quietly, "He's lying."

"Think so?"

"Yeah. Let's not stay for supper, hombre," Earl suggested in an undertone.

Shell tipped his own glass up, emptying it. As he drank it to the suds, he glanced around, noticing that the peasants and the Americans who had occupied the other tables were now gone.

There were three tough looking Mexicans standing at the bar. None of them had a drink in his hand or one on the counter. Paco was a little to their left, hands beneath the counter.

"Things are shaping up," Shell said, putting his glass down.

"We'd better take our chances now," Earl said, putting his hat on. "There might be more of 'em on the way." He smiled to Paco and held up his glass as if asking for a refill. When Paco turned a quarter away, Earl shouted: "Now!"

Earl had his pistol up and firing before any other man could react. The tall man at the center of the bar gasped, stepped back and stumbled. Shell saw the flow of blood soaking his white shirt front.

Earl fired again and Shell crouched, moving right. His Colt was in his hand and he and Earl touched off together as the gunmen at the bar also drew.

"Shell felt a bullet whine past his ear and thud into the wall. He took his time, wanting a clean shot. Shelter thumbed back his hammer twice, getting two round into the bandit on the right.

The badman staggered, tried to lift his pistol and squeezed the trigger, firing into the floor. Paco had ducked, wheeling away, now he reappeared behind the screen of rolling black powder smoke, shotgun in his massive fists.

Earl was swaying on his feet, and Shell swung his Colt toward Paco, firing as the scattergun exploded, filling the room with the roar of thunder.

There was one killer standing yet and Shell went to his knee, firing in return as the outlaw triggered a shot which plowed up the wood of the table beside Morgan.

The man screamed with pain, grabbed at his throat and slid to a seated position on the bar room floor. Paco was down, sobbing with pain. The others were dead.

"Let's get the hell out of here!" Earl shouted.

He was hit, Shell could see that now. His pantleg leaked blood, his face was grim. The acrid smell of burnt gunpowder hung heavy in the room. Shell slipped an arm around Earl's waist and they hobbled to the door of the cantina, Shell's Colt covering their retreat.

Outside there was a crowd, but they took to their heels when the two Americans burst through the saloon doors. Shell untied the horses, hoisting Bentley into the saddle where he clung to the pommel, face ashen.

"You going to make it?"

"I'll make it," Earl snarled. "Use those damned spurs!"

Shell wheeled the chestnut around and took the main street at a dead run, leading the black. Earl was on his heels, holding on like a straw man. A lone shot from some upstairs room followed them wildly.

They wound up and across the brushy mesa. Earl was losing plenty of blood and the riding was doing him no good. He angrily refused a suggestion that they rest.

"We keep up this pace," Shell told him soberly, "you'll never have to worry about Twyner."

"I know a place," Earl panted. "Old prospector's shack. Half a mile."

Earl led the way again. It was a tricky, sloping path which dipped into a ravine then climbed nearly five hundred feet to the rimrock. Back along a stand of oak, deep in a hollow was the dilapidated hut.

Earl would have fallen from the saddle, but Shell caught him and carried him to the door, kicking it open. A packrat darted from the light and Shell walked through the heavy cobwebs to the cot which remained, aged leather straps strung between rough timbers.

"I'll see to your leg."

"Hide the horses," Earl coughed.

"Your leg first," Shell said. He slit the pantleg as Earl lay back, breathing heavily. "It's clean," he told Bentley. "Right on through the meat."

With his silk scarf Shell plugged up the hole on either side, bandaging it tightly with his shirt tail. There was no guarantee the leg would heal clean, but at least it would stop the bleeding, and Earl had lost plenty of it. His boot was filled with dry, sticky blood.

Shell slid his boots off and covered him with the blanket from his roll. Then he led the horses deeper into the oak woods and picketed them where there was grass.

Earl was sleeping, feverish when Shell returned with their gear. Shell knocked the grounds out of their coffee pot and started boiling some water, digging the pack rat's nest out of the ancient stone stove the prospector had constructed, flushing the wren's nests out of the flue.

He shaved some jerky with his bowie, making a thin, salty soup. Earl opened deeply hooded eyes as Shell brought it to him. Feverish eyes, they watched Shell cautiously.

"I can't ride," Earl whispered.

"You'll be up in a few days," Shell said with little confidence. The blood Earl's body could replace. If an infection developed . . . it could be bad. He gave Earl a sip of the soup.

"A few days . . . and where'll you be?" he demanded.

"I'll be right here, Earl."

"I'm holding you back." Earl was thoughtful, silent. Why would Morgan wait for him, nurse him? He had told the man all there was to know about Twyner's hideout. Even when he was able to ride, Earl knew he would be in no shape to fight, climb . . . "Why?"

"I'd get lonesome," Shell said without smiling.

"Butterfield could have done worse," Earl said quietly. Then his head sagged back and he fell off to sleep. Shell noticed the muzzle of Bentley's gun protruding from under the blanket. It was clenched in his hand, ready.

Shell found a battered tin pot in the corner and

he scrubbed it out, throwing a handful of coffee into two cups of water. When that was boiled he put the fire out, not wanting to let it burn longer than necessary.

Twyner knew they were in Mexico and might be looking for them. Who knew where Thumb was.

Shell took his coffee outside, moving through the cool night to a position higher up, on an exposed ledge. He sat there the night long, eyes alert, watching the slender thread of trail which led to the cabin.

Shelter had dozed off, for only a moment it seemed, and when his eyes blinked open the sun was rising, a reddish halo preceding it. It was quiet below, and Shell stretched luxuriantly, taking the kinks out of his night-cramped muscles.

Earl was awake, feverish when Shelter entered the cabin. He spoke, but much of it was incoherent. Once his eyes locked on Shell's and he said clearly, "I would have killed you, you know. It was Drusilla—she liked you, she wanted you to live."

"She was a good woman," Shell answered. He had reheated the soup, but Earl went under again before he could feed him any of it.

He was like that the rest of the day and through the night, drifting in and out, babbling about folks and places which Shell knew nothing about. All Morgan could do was try to keep his fevered body cool, and give him sips of the broth when he was able to take them.

He changed the dressing on Earl's leg, relieved

208

to find it bruised, raw, but apparently not gangrenous. Shell had taken a leg off with a Bowie knife once, he had no desire to ever attempt it again.

At night he sat on the ledge again, watching for movement, smoke. But there was none. He itched to be moving, hoping against hope that Twyner was holed up, and not moving himself.

Earl was sitting up the next day, but still obviously unable to travel. He was able to eat, however, and ravenously hungry. Shell fried some beef and made some sourdough in a pan. It was burned, but it bothered Earl none at all. The outlaw seemed grateful, but unable to accept Shell's help for what it was. Made suspicious by his years on the outlaw trail, he probed for an answer.

Once he said out of the blue, "You mean to kill Twyner?"

"If I have to," Shell answered, turning from the stove. "I'd sooner take him to Pueblo and see him tried for those stage holdups."

Shell studied Earl, trying to get a lead on what he was really after. He didn't give a damn about Twyner, obviously.

"Then that gold—you'd be needing it for evidence, wouldn't you?" Earl asked quietly.

"It wouldn't hurt," Shell replied. So there it was. Earl was still fishing, still not believing Shell entirely. To Bentley's way of thinking everyone had an ulterior motive. And to Earl's mind there was no one, *no one* who would not grab at fifty thousand in gold.

Again and again that day and the next they went over Twyner's fortress hideout, Earl drawing diagrams of the stronghold on the wall with a charred stick.

"That's somethin'," Shell whistled. "Makes Lookout Mountain look like a piece of cake."

"And we won't be having any artillery," Earl said. "I think the place was originally an Indian cliff house," he said in answer to Shell's questions. "There are a few others in that area.

"The Major, he dynamited the remains of the Indian house out . . . the Indians, you understand have been gone for centuries. They were the original people of the desert. Not like the Apache, the Navajo. Hell, I was talking to a man who went to college up in Canada. He tells me the Apache came from up there. They drifted slowly southward, fighting and being fought off until they come this far south.

"It was the Apache, some guess, that killed off the original people—the old ones, as they say."

The stronghold Earl sketched was a two story house of adobe over poles, set a hundred feet up the sheer face of a red cliff. The house was set back in a notch which had either been dynamited or cut away by the original inhabitants so that it completely shielded the house from above as well as below.

"How does he get up?" Shell wanted to know.

"Originally there was only a series of notched poles stretched from ledge to ledge. The Major, he put a kind of a catwalk up. Iron driven into the cliffs, with plank suspension walks. Usually there's three, four men on lookout. They're up there high, perched waiting. They can pick you off before you know what's happening.''

And from above?'' Shell wanted to know. Earl lifted his eyes frowning.

"Can't be done. There's a hundred feet or so above, and no ledge to land on, the house recessed like it is. You'd have to be a hawk to make it.''

"It's the only way," Shell told him. "Scale that butte." He sketched it on the wall, Earl studying it. "Drop your loop on a big rock, a dead tree, whatever you can find, then skin on down your line.''

"It can't be done! You'd have to swing away out to get your pendulum motion up. Then . . . hell, you'd have to jump, hoping to land on the roof. Hoping nobody saw you, that you didn't land right in their laps. Nobody can do that.''

"How do you reckon the Apaches did it in the first place?'' Shell asked, lifting an eyebrow.

"That way . . . maybe. Maybe they just starved 'em out. Hell, I don't know, Morgan. All I know is it's impossible for us.''

"If you've got a better idea, Earl, you'd better lay it out to me, because I'm fresh out of ideas. If this won't work," he tapped the wall, "we've got nothing.''

"Say those old time Apaches did do it this way—and I'm not convinced of it. *They* dropped more than one man. One's all I got . . . I can't climb. Say you get in there, Shelter," Earl said, his eyes dark, worried, "just how the hell do you plan on getting *out?*"

Now that was another matter, and one that would take some serious considering. Most serious.

17.

Aguila was an isolated backwater fifteen miles to the south and west where nothing much had ever been, and nothing worth building would ever likely be built. There was a general store there, however, run by a man named McMurty who had run across the border twenty years before with some trouble on his heels, and married a Mexican sheepherder's daughter and settled down.

Earl Bentley sat his horse in the rutted rust

colored alley behind the store while Shell went in.

McMurty, a huge, bearded man with one twinkling blue eye glanced up from the counter. A naked, dark haired boy of no more than two scooted through a side door as Shell entered.

McMurty looked Shell up and down, adjusting the patch over his eye. He nodded, "Where's your partner?" the storekeeper asked.

"Partner?"

"Maybe it wasn't you," McMurty said. "Heard two Americanos shot up Paco's place in La Paloma. I've been expectin' they'd ride through."

"I need a hat," Shell said, skirting the matter. "Wind must've got mine. Straw . . . that'll do," he said as McMurty picked up a sombrero and showed it to him.

Shell tried it on and glanced in the chip of a mirror McMurty had fastened to the wall.

"How about a poncho?" McMurty asked, that blue eye bright with amusement. "Looks like the wind got your coat too."

He handed Shell a brightly striped poncho and Shell slipped it on, nodding his approval.

"Now then, thing I mostly came for was some rope. Hemp will do." Shell added, "Nearly round-up time."

"Sure. How much, cowboy?"

"Say a hundred and fifty feet. No splices."

"A hundred and . . . you must throw a wide loop, *hombre!*"

"I've been known to," Shell answered with a smile.

"Let me measure it out of the barrel. I might have to throw a splice in it, though, that's a lot of rope. If I do, don't you worry none. You'll not see a splice of McMurty's giving before the virgin rope does."

As it happened he did have a hundred and fifty feet, barely and he flopped it on the counter in two heavy coils. "That's a load just to carry," McMurty said. He scratched some figures on the counter and totalled them.

Shell walked to the door, McMurty beside him. The rope Shell loaded onto the chestnut, he was riding the black now. McMurty lifted a hand as Shell turned his pony up the main street.

"Watch those big steers, cowboy!" McMurty called after him. "They carry big horns."

They rode into the low hills east of Aguila, aiming for the big red mountain beyond the mesa. The land here was ancient, and perhaps that thumb of a mountain was all that remained of the original mesa which was collapsed and broken by time and earth movements.

There were *calderas* here, cinder cones which had outlived the ancient volcanoes which bred them. The ground was lava rich, both black lava and red, and the growth was sparse—yucca, cholla with here and there a deep blue-green paloverde.

Yet there was water, in isolated pockets. It seemed artesian in nature, as Shell could see no upland source and the water was clear, sweet.

They sat on a knoll some thousand feet above Aguila which appeared only as a dark smear against the pervading red of the countryside. The mountain loomed over them, and Earl looked at it uncertainly.

"I'm not even sure you can get up that, let alone down the far side," he commented.

The red rock mountain was rough, wind cut and fluted. Ancient rock, the entire mountain seemed ready to crumble, although it had survived the centuries and would survive for eons more. Nothing grew along all those long flanks, except here and there a tenacious nopal cactus.

The wind was swirling where they stood now, up above it could be treacherous, yet it had to be scaled, and by nightfall if possible. Night on that peak could bring sudden death.

"I won't be much help from here on out," Earl said. "It's all up to you, Morgan. That," he nodded, "is your mountain to climb."

"You just be there when I come down," Shell said. "I'll be hung out to dry if you're not waiting for me."

"You know I'll be waiting," Earl said, "if you bring down that gold."

When the horses could go no farther, Shell threw the poncho back across his shoulders, out of the way and took up the huge coils of rope, with his sombrero hanging down his back he moved off afoot toward the mountain peak, glancing once across his shoulder to see Earl give the thumb's-up before he turned back, leading the three spare horses.

It was cold, coming dark now, and Morgan was on his own. The rope rested uncomfortably around his neck and shoulders and at the first chance he paused to fashion a rough pack out of the rope itself and his poncho before resuming the climb.

Shell moved cautiously upward, racing the approaching night. The wind buffeted his back, standing his hair on end. Still, the weathered peak lent itself to climbing. So much of it was broken, crumbled, jagged that it was not difficult to find outcroppings to rest a boot on, handholds.

Only twice did one of these handholds break loose, the second time leaving Shell perilously dangling by one hand, the ground far below, but he made it.

Exhausted, dripping with sweat, he crawled up onto the gently sloping mountain peak while sunset still reddened the land. He threw down the rope and rubbed his aching shoulders, taking deep gulping breaths, trying to stretch the kinks from his knotted leg muscles.

He stood a thousand feet above the high desert, watching sundown fizzle before the coming shadows, the constant wind washing over him.

"So much for the easy part," he told himself.

He wanted to sit, to rest, but knew there was no time for it. He must cross the mountain and locate the cliff house before darkness. Already he was shaving it fine.

Shelter hefted his rope and moved out, walking across the barren, wind-swept butte. All around him below was desert. Red splotches spread out from the base of the butte, from the broken mesa near La Paloma only to be swallowed up by the eternal yellow sands. The butte itself cast a long shadow across the land.

The landmark he looked for was a notch in the eastern rimrock. Yet he could not find it. From below it seemed large, definite, according to Earl at least. But from above Shell could not make it out. Not in this light.

He had crossed to the eastern face and he eased himself forward, peering down. It took his breath away. Sheer it was, utterly smooth, worn down by the winds, perhaps. There was nothing of the fortress to be seen.

Shell stood again, rubbing his forehead. He searched left for a quarter of a mile, still not finding the notch which should be directly above the house. Then he went the other way, nearly losing his footing once in the near total darkness.

And then he found it. It was not a notch in the rimrock as it must appear from below, but a notched knob protruding from the wall of the butte some fifty feet down the face of the cliff.

This was it then . . . Shell threw his rope coils to the ground, wondering what caused a man to go this far. What madness is in us? He found a huge white boulder to anchor his rope and he tied to it, flipping the line out of the coils into a straight line.

Standing on the edge of the precipice he fed the line into the abyss at his feet, the wind still gnawing at his poncho, his trousers.

The wind played with the long line as well, but

it was heavy and whipped only a little. Shelter pulled on his gloves, testing the anchor once before he went over.

Shell had the rope wrapped once around his waist, his left hand behind him. As he dropped into space, he kicked off the rock letting out the slack. Landing again, he bent his knees and pushed off once more.

He was down two hundred feet when a gust of wind caught him. Kicking off, he was twisted around so that his back slammed into the butte face, knocking the breath from his body.

Shell muttered a curse, hanging on where he rested until his breath returned, the lights stopped blinking inside his skull.

Then again he descended, his kick-outs shorter, more methodical. It was pitch black below now, and Shell, try as he might, could pick up nothing that looked like the recess where the house sat.

A sudden sobering thought came to him—suppose that had not been the proper location to descend? Did he have the strength to climb back up?

But he still had slack hanging far below and he crept down, his boots only now and again trickling gravel below as he contacted the stone.

And then it was there.

Arcing out, Shell had flexed his legs, expecting to come back to the butte, but instead he swung in, past the face of the rock, and at the same moment he saw a patch of something white.

He hung dead on the line for a long minute,

twisting around to try to see what lay below. After a time the roof of the adobe house could be made out—far to the left.

Yet there was a crescent of ledge just below him. Not four feet wide, it sent a shiver up Shell's spine to realize *that* was where he would have to land.

The ledge was away from him twenty feet or so, and Shell slowly began rocking, moving with the slow rhythm of a pendulum. As he swung he eased himself slightly down, measuring the ledge. Closer he swung.

His boots scraped the ledge, but he was yanked away by the line. He could not let go of the line until he was sure of a foothold; could not be sure of a foothold without releasing the line.

All of his concentration was fixed on that narrow outcropping, tantalizingly close, incredibly distant. He swung toward it, balked, swung back. Now he was able to push off the ledge as the line arced farther in and Shell did so, dropping the rope with his back hand, letting the line unwind from around his waist.

His hands were cramped, his shoulders felt as if they were being pulled from their sockets. Hanging on as he was now, there was little time for deciding. He would inexorably slip downward, away from the ledge as he weakened.

Shell swung in, felt his boots finding the ledge, and he let the line fall free. His hands clawed at the stone wall, finding no grip, and he teetered on the ledge.

His feet slipped, and he tightroped a way,

throwing himself to the ledge. He grabbed for a handhold, found one and lay there gripping it tenaciously, his left arm and leg dangling in space. Slowly, his heart pounding like a drum, ears ringing with the rush of blood, soaked through with perspiration, Shell got to his feet, back to the wall.

There it was—the Fortress Twyner. A beautiful, two-story adobe with red tile. Pole supports protruded through the outside walls. All of the windows were in the second story, all were barred.

"If the Major had fought the war the way he fights his private battles . . ." Shell smiled grimly. He stood stock still a long minute, searching the ledge, or what he could see of it.

Behind and up there was the remains of an ancient cliff dwelling, carved into the red stone. There were two low outbuildings, one near enough to the house that Shell thought he could reach one of those upstairs windows by leaping from the roof.

Throwing back his poncho to have his Colt more readily at hand, he moved through the shadows, eyes cutting for movement, for light on metal, for a human silhouette. It was silent, cold. The breath fogged from Shell's lips as he made the outbuilding.

He shinnied to the roof and stood looking up at the barred window. There was no light visible through the curtains, but that was heavy material of some kind, and there was no guarantee the room was actually empty.

221

There was no choice. Shell jumped, caught the black iron with his hands and skinned on up. There was a latch on the grate, but it was cast metal and when Shell rapped it with his gun butt, it cracked away. He swung it open on a squeaky hinge and tried the window itself. Open. He swung up and in, slipping his Colt from his belt as he landed.

The room was hardly empty.

Alicia sat there soaking in her bath tub, an amused smile on her full lips.

18.

"Well," she said, cool as you please, "come in. But you can put the gun away. As you see, I am unarmed."

That was a fact, and she was definitely concealing nothing. As Shell watched she stepped from the tub crossing the room. She moved with a fluid grace, and there was not an ounce of fat on her body, only firm, tantalizing flesh.

Alicia picked up a towel and began patting herself dry. "Is that door locked?" he asked.

"Yes. I don't invite *everyone* to my baths," she said coolly. "How did *you* get here, Mister Morgan?" Alicia asked. "Oh—the dynamite shack. I've asked the Major a hundred times to have it moved. I always thought it was dangerous . . . but not in this way."

Shell did not respond to her smile, fetching as it was. A single word had lodged in his mind, "Dynamite?"

"Yes—it's stored in the shed below my window. The Major said it's perfectly safe, but I . . ." Alicia read Shell's thoughts, partially and she broke off.

"I've never seen a more determined man," she said. Slowly she dressed, slipping into a loose chemise and then a long dark colored gown. "But I think you'd better leave while you can. He'll be coming here shortly, you know?"

"The Major? Here. What for?"

"You can't guess?" Alicia smiled as she said it, but Shell thought it was a bitter smile. Her eyes were dark, not reflecting the smile.

"Why do you stay with him?" Shell blurted out.

"Major Twyner?" she shrugged. "The money. I have a family, my mother and three sisters. Once we were well to do, but unfortunately my father was French, Mister Morgan. After the otherthrow of Maximilian he was shot, our possessions confiscated. What else was there to be done?"

"He's good to you?" Shell wanted to know.

Her eyes suddenly lost that composure, "He's

a swine!" she snapped. She turned her back to Shell, brushing her hair in a huge gilt-framed mirror. "You'd better go," Alicia said quietly.

"I'm leaving. Soon. But the Major's going with me. You'd better plan on leaving too, Alicia. I'm afraid there won't be much to stay here for when I'm done."

"They'll kill you."

"Maybe."

"Why?" she asked, glancing at Shelter in the mirror.

"He's a swine," Shell said, and she smiled faintly.

"I can't help you," Alicia said frankly.

"I'm not asking for your help. I understand how it is." As much as the woman might despise Twyner, he was the support of Alicia's family, and she knew him for a butcher. Shell neither wanted nor expected her help.

"You're quite a man," she said, studying this long, rough featured blond man in the mirror. "I hope he does not kill you."

"I won't go easy," Shell said. "You just be ready to travel, and if there's shooting get away from me."

"All right." She said it hesitantly and Shell frowned slightly, wanting to trust her, afraid to.

Alicia crossed the room to her canopied bed. There she lounged, watching Shell, the door to the hallway beyond. Curiously, without saying a word, she watched as Morgan went back out the open window, reappearing a few minutes later.

Whatever else she was, Alicia was a cool one.

She calmly watched as Shell took up a position in the far corner, behind the door.

He waited impatiently. There was little to do but feast his eyes on the girl on the bed, and he did so. Long-legged, her gown was drawn up to her thighs, Her breasts were full, nearly free of the gown, her hips promising . . .

Theré was a knock at the door and Alicia rose, gliding across the room. Shell heard a muttered word, and his hand tensed on his Colt. Alicia re-entered the room, arms outstretched, drawing him in.

When the Major was inside Shell leaped for the door, slammed it shut and locked it, his back to the door, Colt levelled on the Major's guts.

"Morgan!" He sputtered, not finding words strong enough. He was dressed in trousers and shirtsleeves, wearing his glasses. His eyes went from Alicia to Shell, to the gun.

"Thought I'd drop in," Shell said.

"How did you get here?"

"I was hiding in her skirts," Shell said quietly. Twyner was furious, but he didn't have that fear etched on his face, the fear of a man facing death. He was downright smug.

"You can't get out of here. Why don't you give it up now, I'll let you go."

"Not likely, Major. I've waited too long."

"I'll say one thing, Morgan, you've got balls, but there's no way. No way," he shook his head, "they'll shoot you to dog meat."

"Not if they're smart," Shell said calmly. "Not unless they want the whole damned mountain coming down on them." To Twyner's quizzical expression, Shell pulled his poncho aside and showed him the twenty sticks of dynamite tied around his waist, a fuse protruding from the neat bundle.

"You're insane!" Twyner stared at the bundle.

"Could be."

"One bullet . . .!"

"If it comes, you'll be standing there next to me, watching Major." Shell waved his pistol. "We're leaving now. You too, Alicia. If you got any regard left for your own life, Twyner, you'll keep your dogs off me, because we're in this together, sir."

"All right . . ." Twyner was trying to be cool, unsuccessfully. Shell's own mouth was dry, his nerves raw. Of them all only Alicia seemed truly calm, as tranquil as if they were heading for a garden stroll. She was slipping into her boots.

"We're taking that Butterfield gold with us," Shell said.

Twyner spun furiously, but his look softened with his second look at that Colt. "Don't forget," Shell told him, opening his poncho so that Twyner could clearly see those twenty sticks of dynamite. "If they start shooting there's a good chance you'll be hit, Major. Or that I'll have time to shoot you. Maybe your own men won't hit you . . . maybe they'll just touch fire to the dynamite. I'd handle this real cautiously, were I you."

"All right. But damnit . . ."

"Move!" Shell swung open the door and he

followed Twyner down the long hallway, his Colt beneath his poncho, the sombrero low over his eyes. Alicia trailed after them.

They saw no one. Entering a locked room Twyner went to a big green safe and opened it. The original burlap sack still sat near the safe and he scooped the gold coin into the bag, perspiration glinting on his white forehead.

"Now what?" he asked, standing, offering the bag to Shell.

"You carry that, Major," Shell told him. He wanted his own hands free. "Now," he nodded "we get off this mountain. Quietly, I hope."

They moved down the corridor swiftly, Shell holding the back of the Major's shirt, his cocked pistol jammed into Twyner's spine.

"You can't make it," Twyner said again. "Give it up now."

"Keep moving." Shell jabbed him again, harder yet. The front door was ahead of them now, and an armed outlaw sat slumped in a chair, watching them warily. He was trying to make out Shell, apparently, studying that poncho, the low sombrero. Shell stopped abruptly, holding Twyner back.

"Tell him, Major," Shell hissed. "Now!" Again he poked that muzzle into Twyner's back and the Major spoke.

"Put your gun away, Carlos."

"Huh?" The outlaw shook his head, not liking it.

"Put your damned gun away! This man's got a gun on me and enough dynamite strapped on him to bring the house down on our heads."

"Mebbe the mountain as well," Shell said in a low voice, and Carlos shucked his gun, tossing it across the room. "Fine," Shell said. "Now step aside, Carlos. Alicia, open that door."

She did as she was told and as the door swung open Shell saw two other men, a little ways from the house. They were talking, smoking, their cigarettes making tiny red sparks of light.

"Don't say anything," Shell said in a low voice. "If they talk, just tell them it's all right, understand?"

"I understand." The Major's face was glossed with cold sweat.

"Good. Which way down?"

"Over there," the Major nodded.

Alicia—you move out first," Shell said, and she did so, walking calmly, arms crossed.

They were a good five hundred feet up. The empty, moon-silvered desert spread out in all directions. Shell could see the way down now. A sort of platform, of iron was just beyond a waist-high gate. From there, iron supported catwalks zig-zagged down the cliff to a second level.

"What's down there?" Shell demanded.

"The horses. From there a man can ride," the Major puffed. He was carrying that gold, and it was a load for him. He staggered ahead of Shell, the two outlaws watching them.

Finally one threw his butt away and took half a dozen steps toward them. "Everything all right, Major Twyner?"

"Fine, Wes," the Major replied, but the outlaw

looked uncertain.

"Who the hell's that with you?" he asked, peering into the darkness.

"Go on back," the Major said. He was in a real sweat now. He hadn't forgotten that dynamite for a moment. "Everything's all right."

The outlaw shrugged and spun on his heel. "Good," Shell said, "you're doing fine, Major. Let's get on down the catwalk now, shall we?"

Alicia had kept on walking, she was already at the second landing, walking in the other direction on a lower level. Shell followed Twyner down the long plank walk, eyes going to the darkness.

They had reached the second landing before they saw anyone. Standing above them at the lookout post was a guard, the rifle in his hand catching the glint of moonlight.

"Major?" It was Shields and his eyes narrowed briefly, a savage, twisted smile forming moments later. "Morgan!"

Shields had always been quick on the shoot, and he was anxious this time as well. He drew his Winchester to his shoulder, still smiling.

"No! God, Shields!" the Major screamed, holding up a hand, but there was no restraining the gunman.

Alicia took off at a run, Shell shoved Twyner, hard, and brought his Colt up from beneath his poncho, firing from the hip. Shield's grin exploded into a mask of pain as Shell's bullet caught the outlaw high in the chest, wheeling him around.

Still Shields was determined, however, and

230

with his mouth filled with blood, his legs shaky, he levered three quick shots through his repeater, spraying the mountainside around Shell before Shields toppled forward, bouncing off the rocks as he fell into the abyss.

Shields' shots had triggered off a war. Riflemen perched above opened fire, strafing the rocks. Angry ricochets whined off the cliff into space.

They fired blindly, aiming at the spot where Shelter's guns had stabbed flame, but he was no longer there. Diving headlong, he had rolled twenty feet farther down the catwalk.

Twyner was running as fast as he could, and Shell got to his feet, drawing the fire of other guns up on the rim. A bullet stung the iron rail near his hand, a second exploded under his feet, splintering the catwalk. Shell took off at a run, firing over his shoulder.

Bullets sang at his heels as he dove for the platform, crawling behind a rock. A guard just overhead loomed up and Shell swung around, firing off-handedly. The gunman's face disappeared behind a gory mask of blood and he lurched forward, sliding down the rocks.

They had him pinned down from above. Anxiously Shell looked down the catwalk to see Twyner nearing the stable. He fired a chance shot in the Major's direction. A shot he did not cut too fine, knowing Alicia was there, and answering guns tore at the rock around Shelter from the stable.

Shell saw a man running along the rim and he

fired. The silhouette disappeared, hit or not Shell could not say. But there were too many to fight off for long. Above and below now the guns rang out, filling the night with the roar of thunder.

Shell yanked the dynamite free of its restraining tie and held it up, firing his .44 just beside the fuse to no avail. Again, rapidly he fired and this time the flying particles of black gunpowder caught fire to the fuse.

It hissed angrily, yellow sparks dancing as Shell stepped out and heaved it as far as he could. He watched as the dynamite bundle disappeared over the ledge. Then, running in a crouch, he came out of his hiding place, emptying his pistol, trying to keep their fire off him as he dashed crazily for the stable.

A man above Shell reared suddenly up. He had been lying flat on the dark knob of rock, and now he came to his feet, rifle ready.

It was then that the dynamite caught and the world exploded in a flash of red. The outlaw above Shell was blown off the rock into space. Above him, near the house someone screamed.

Flame rolled over the house, and the mountain shuddered. Smoke billowed up and a second explosion—possibly the dynamite shed tore the night apart. It was as bright as day, everything washed with crimson and brilliant yellow, a man ran insanely along the ledge, disappearing in a cloud of smoke.

The second explosion threatened to tear the mountain apart. The catwalk swayed wildly under Shell's feet and he grabbed for the rail as the iron anchors were torn loose by the force of the explosions. The catwalk snapped free at one end and Shelter's feet went out from under him.

With a terrible groaning sound the catwalk sagged downward, Shelter clinging desperately to it as a shock wave washed over him, the flash from the flame searing his face. His ears were filled with undying thunder.

He hung precariously in space, a twisted iron rail some fifty feet long dangling him like a bass on a line. The house was afire, the flames leaping against the cold sky. And the mountain groaned with the explosion. A third muffled explosion followed moments later and Shell was tossed like a leaf. Still he clung to the iron railing, desperately searching for a way down.

Down—there was no way down, only upwards. Hand over hand, face streaked with the flames, Shell worked upward, trying to reach the catwalk below him. It would be a drop of thirty feet or so, but if he did not break a leg, he might make it. If the guns in the stable didn't chop him down before that.

Grunting with the exertion he reached the point above the next level of catwalk. The mountain shuddered and the flames continued unabated. Shell let go and dropped to the catwalk, landing hard.

The breath was knocked out of him, and he could feel that something was not right with his ankle. But there was no time to concern himself with that. He hobbled downward, frantically reloading his colt as he approached the stable.

Panting, he slid up beside the stable wall, and turning he kicked open the side door, rolling inside. Empty.

It could not be, but it was.

The Major had a horse under him and was making his run, the men from the stable with him. There were no other horses.

Shell muttered an oath and rushed for the main door, flinging it open. Nothing. From the stable a long, dark road wound down to the desert floor.

He hesitated for a moment, but another deafening explosion from above decided him and he started down the winding trail, hopping as much as running because of the ankle which was now shot through with pain, every step down like grinding glass into the joint.

He ran for as long as he could, then panting, he stopped, leaning against a huge boulder where the road made a sharp bend. Looking back he could see what remained of the house: wildly dancing flames which sent clouds of billowing black smoke into the night sky. A part of the butte had come down, smothering the rear of the house with earth and rock, and only there did it not burn.

He saw no other man, heard nothing above the distant crackling flames. He rose, cold, damp with perspiration, ankle shot through with pain, and walked on, breathing deeply.

The desert was black, empty for as far as he could see by the light of the smoke-screened moon. An owl, perched deep in the chapparal hooted twice and then was silent. There was nothing else but the scent of the dust from long gone horses.

The horseman approached at a walk as Shelter watched him. A dark silhouette in the saddle, Earl Bentley said dryly, "Maybe that plan of yours didn't work out entirely . . . but damned if you don't make a show of it, Shelter."

Earl lifted his eyes to the house, the flames lighting his hard, chiseled features. "Damned if you don't make a show of it!"

Shell came forward, hobbling a bit. "See the Major?" he wanted to know.

"Saw him. I figured he'd run south, into Mexico, though. The son of a bitch is headed back toward the border. I was at the wrong end of the canyon."

"All right." Shell lifted Earl's canteen and drank deeply, pouring a trickle down his shirt. "His army's cut up some now, Earl. He can't have more'n two, three men with him. Figure we can take him?"

Earl smiled faintly, "I figure," he said. "How about you?"

"We won't know till we try," Shell said, swinging onto the black horse. "But I figure so—let's have at it."

19.

They rode to the north throughout the night, riding hard, switching horses frequently to keep a fresh mount under them. Twyner would not be stopping to rest, to eat, to drink, and they did not either.

Earl was silent, intent; his leg seemed to bother him but a little now. They were not a mile from the border still riding due north, pursuing the tracks which Twyner and his men had scored in the drift sand, when the night gave way to the rising, red sun; and they pushed themselves even harder as the morning made the tracking easier.

They slowed the pace a little to keep from killing the horses—did Twyner have that much sense? He should have, but the man was in a panic, thinking only of escape, and probably not of the horses.

Twyner meant to make it a long hard run, and he was doing just that. From their tracks, however, Shelter could plainly read the vital fact that Twyner had no spare horses with him.

"I believe he'll kill them ponies," Earl said as he stretched out a hand to take the canteen from Shell.

"Looks like," Morgan replied.

They were riding at an easy pace. The sun was rising, but there was a cooling breeze, and it was not so hot as it had been.

"The damn fool won't let no other horse tote that gold but his," Earl pointed out. In the soft sand it was plain to read—Twyner's horse, carrying that extra load cut much deeper tracks. Tracks which had not varied since the trail began.

There were four horses ahead of them. All of them ridden. That meant Twyner, Alicia and two gunhands. With luck Shell figured they should come up on them within an hour. Maybe sooner if their horses foundered, and there was every indication they might.

Here and there you could see where a horse misstepped. They were being ridden at a fast pace with a heavy load and no water. It came to

Shell in a flash.

He's got to be planning on getting fresh horses somewhere near," Shell said and Earl's lips tightened. It was true, had to be. The Major was many things—a fool, no. "Got any ideas?" Shelter asked.

"Yes, damnit! Mendoza's farm . . . if I'd thought of it sooner . . . damn!"

"Which way?"

"Follow them tracks," Earl said tersely. "We missed the cut-off trail."

Now Shelter was worried. Their own horses were doing well, switching off as they had been, but there was no way they would keep up with fresh ponies for any distance. He kneed the black, urging it to a faster pace than he liked.

The land was a series of low rolling dunes with scattered greasewood and cholla, ahead lay the box canyon where Mendoza's farm was located.

"Farm" was a loose term. Mendoza was a wanted man on either side of the border, and he raised little on his farm but the bottle. But the place was one in a chain of outlaw stations where horses could be swapped. If there were any other men there was anyone's guess. They could be riding into a nest of outlaws, something neither of them was up to just now.

Shell was feeling some of his hurts. His face, scorched in the explosion, was bothering him although he wore his sombrero as low as possible to keep the sun's heat off. His ankle was swollen inside his boot, stiff, painful; and his hands which had been sunburned, stomped and cut were now blistered on the palms—the result of the rope climbing.

Earl's leg was still leaking blood. There was a dark splotch on the gray of his pantleg. The horses they rode were weary, and the ammunition had gotten low.

To top it the wind was rising and the sand had begun swirling about, getting into their eyes, nostrils. Earl pulled his bandana up over his face; Shell no longer had a bandana, and he had to be content with keeping his head low.

They rode silently through the screen of wind-whipped sand. Shell's mouth was dry and to open it meant a mouthful of sand.

They rode on across the endless desert, pursuing death at a steady pace. It was growing more difficult to see as the wind picked up even more and a sandstorm built. Now, through a brief parting of the sand clouds, Shell could see gray canyon walls beside the trail. Nothing was visible ahead and even Earl's horse was difficult to make out.

The sand peppered ears, necks, any exposed piece of skin like birdshot. Their nostrils and ears were clotted with the stuff. Breathing was difficult, seeing impossible.

"I think we're almost there!" Earl shouted above the wind, his hand on Shell's arm.

"Is there another way out of this canyon?" Shell hollered back. The wind, shrieking in the canyon, bent his words so that he had to lean close and repeat the question.

"No! No other way!"

Then Twyner would have to ride past them if he were to make a run. Could he slip past unseen? Possible—the sand rolled past in huge, wind-driven waves, swirling, cutting out the sun.

Yet horses and men had suffocated in such sandstorms, most likely the Major would have to sit tight inside of Mendoza's shack, although that would chafe him.

"We got to get out of this wind!" Shell shouted. He choked and ducked his head inside his poncho.

"There!" Earl tapped his shoulder and they moved toward the south, finding a small cubbyhole where the brunt of the wind was cut. The sand still swirled, and seeing was difficult, but at least a man could breath. Shell slid from the saddle, gasping.

From there they could see the shack, the sand allowing. A squat, slope roofed structure of weathered gray wood it sat up against the canyon walls, shaded by a trio of huge old sycamores.

Shell took a drink of the canteen, shaking it as he handed it to Earl. "Last swallow," Shelter told him.

Earl nodded bleakly and drank it down. His face was a mask of sand and perspiration, his eyebrows and hair frosted with clinging sand. Shell could imagine what he himself looked like.

Together they sagged against the huge gray boulder behind them, eyes fixed on the shack across the canyon. "Think there's anyone else down there?" Earl asked.

Shell searched the house, the grounds slowly, as much as he could through the constant sand. He could only shrug. There was no way of knowing.

It was miserably hot, difficult to breathe. Sweat trickled slowly down Shell's throat and chest. It was Earl who said it, echoing Shell's thoughts:

"We've got to go on in."

"So it seems."

"Are you up to it?" Earl asked, studying the haggard features of the big blond man, the weary red eyes.

"No," Shell answered with barely a smile. "Are you?"

"No." Earl shook his head. He sat holding his wounded thigh.

"Let's get a gettin'," Shell said wryly. He stepped toward his horse. "If we wait till we're up to it, he'll be long gone."

There was no way to come up unseen on the house—Mendoza had chosen his site well. But with the shifting sand there was a fair chance they could make the next low rise which had a stand of wind brushed salt cedar growing on it.

From there it would be more than chancy, and Shell doubted they could wait the Major out. Inside they would have supplies enough to last a good long while.

Leaving the spare horses in the feeder canyon Earl and Shelter rode slowly into the sandy wash, again taking the full driving force of the sandstorm's fury. It was smothering, all-obscuring, yet it was just what they needed now.

The storm would cover their movements, yet it was no sure thing. The sand had a way of parting at unexpected moments, leaving a clear field of vision. If it parted now, Shell had every reason to expect a hail of gunfire from Mendoza's shack.

It held long enough for them to make the rise, leaving the horses concealed in the gulley. The cedar, sand coated, swaying wildly in the turbulent air, provided shelter, and they lay flat on their bellies, studying the shack where nothing was visible. There was no movement, no horses to be seen, the shack may as well have been empty.

Yet they knew someone had ridden into that canyon—it was empty down there all right, empty as a hornet's nest.

Earl had his Colt in his hand. He turned his head to Shelter. "How do you want to do it?"

"We'd better make our try while the storm holds," Shell answered. "How about the back? Any windows there?"

"I don't think so. I can't recall for sure, I've only been here once."

"I'll try it that way," Shell decided. "When you can't see me anymore, slip in as close as possible to that front door."

Earl nodded and Shell waited until a gust of wind frenzy darkened the earth with a shuddering blast of sand, and he moved. He darted toward the far corner of the shack, the shadows twisting around him.

It was a good hundred yards, and he half expected a bullet at any moment. But the sand-storm held and he made the pole corral beside the house. There was a window on that side of the house, but the angle was bad toward the corral.

He waited a moment longer, the sand stinging him, the wind tearing at his poncho, then he dashed toward the back of the house. One window—up high—and the door which was un-doubtedly bolted and being watched.

Shell pressed flat against the wall of the house, panting for breath. His eyes were raw with the sand, his ankle was on fire with pain.

From where he now stood Shelter could see the horses, tails to the wind, hidden up a small fenced ravine. Had Earl started his move yet?

There were no gunshots so he was still out of sight at least. He waited, counting a slow twenty to give Earl time to creep closer to the front door.

The wind was still building, dark shadows swirled across the yard. It was black as sin at mid-day, hot as hell . . .

Shell turned sharply and kicked the door open. He was met with instant gunfire and he went to a knee, firing himself.

A hatless cowhand with a rifle leaped up and Shell shot him twice, slamming him against the wall behind him. The gunhand staggered and slumped, leaving a smear of blood on the wall as he sank to his knees.

A flurry of shots slammed against the wall beside Shell, showering splinters everywhere and

Shell dove for the table, upending it. Black powder smoke rolled through the room and the sandstorm shrieked in through the open door. There was a half a dozen shots from the front of the house, an answering pop-pop from outside, barely audible above the howl of the wind.

Sand drifted through the room. Shell lifted his head and drew instant fire. A hail of bullets filled the room, several punching through the table top.

Too close. He deserted the table and rushed for the wall beside the next doorway, firing to keep them down. He stood there shovelling fresh loads into the Colt which was hot in his hand.

He crouched and peered into the room. A shot answered that action, but it was high where they had expected him. There were only two men in the room, Shell believed. An outlaw at the window, kept busy by Earl's firing and a huge, black bearded man behind the upturned sofa—Mendoza, probably.

Where then was Twyner? And Alicia.

Mendoza fired twice, tearing the door frame beside Shell's head to bits and Shell returned his fire, watching the big man's head disappear behind the red, moth eaten sofa.

Mendoza came up again, but Shell had been waiting. He fired twice, seeing Mendoza's head snap back, his forehead cave in, then he stepped into the room, gun levelled on the outlaw at the window.

"That's enough," Shell said softly, but the outlaw would have none of it. He spun, an ugly curse filling his mouth and Shell shot him twice low in the chest.

Blood spurted from the man's heart and he toppled forward, dead before he hit the floor.

Mendoza was also dead and Shelter moved quickly through the house. Then he saw it—a side door, open to the wind and sand, and he heard the pounding of hoofs in the front of the house.

He burst from the door, taking a few running strides, in time to see Twyner, Alicia behind him riding hell for leather up the gulley.

Earl appeared beside Shell and he lifted his pistol, taking a lead on Twyner through the sand.

"Don't!" Shell shouted, taking Earl's elbow. "The woman's with him."

"The hell with the woman," Earl snarled, shaking Shelter's hand off. But the storm had swallowed Twyner up and there was nothing left to shoot but wind and sand.

Earl turned savage, fiery eyes toward Shell. "I had him . . .!"

"Get to the horses," Shelter said, slapping his shoulder. Earl hesitated a moment then turned, following Shell to where their horses were tethered.

The storm was in their faces, merciless in its onslaught, as they spurred their horses back up the canyon, Earl reloading even as they rode.

Out on the desert floor the storm was even worse. Walls of sand rose to slap them back. The horses balked, wanting only to turn tail to the driving sand.

They had run a good mile, and they sat letting the horses blow on a low dune. Now and then the curtain of hot sand would part, but they could make out nothing. No shadow not cast by the clouds of sand moved across the desert. There was no sound but the constant shriek of the hot wind.

"I had him," Earl muttered again. Shell glanced at him and answered calmly.

"We'll find him again. He can't make it far with that weight."

"I had him," Earl repeated. Angrily he slapped a hand against his startled horse's neck, moving out onto the flats.

The worst of the storm had blown over within an hour. Still sand moved through the blisteringly hot air, but in thin veils. The blue of the sky could be seen distinctly now.

Still there was no sign of the Major or Alicia. The sand had devoured any tracks. The desert seemed to have swallowed them up. Yet such a thing is not possible, Shelter knew. The man was there. Hiding, in the other direction, suffocated by sand . . . he was there.

Mid-day brought clearing skies and they rode through the debilitating heat like frosted, sun-blistered scarecrows. Northward they rode. The Major had started his run northward, and it was a good bet he would continue that way, into the States.

In which direction? Toward water. There were several sources of water, Pueblo Wells thirty miles to the north and west might be too far in such heat. But there had been water in Carizo when Shell last crossed it. It was no more than ten miles north and east. It was toward Carizo they rode.

Earl sagged in the saddle, morose, half sick. Suddenly, however, he stopped and sat straight. He was pointing at the ground, grinning. Shell rode beside him.

"Looky there!" Earl exulted.

"Be damned."

It was only a single track, cut deeply into some rust colored earth, but it was fresh. The Major's track—they had guessed right.

The horses were weary beneath them, but both men felt fresher now and they pushed on, riding into low hilly country. There were occasional dunes and here and there a beleaguered saguaro cactus frozen against the skyline.

It was late evening when they made Carizo Wash, the horses worn to the nub, the men battered, dehydrated.

Water gushed from an upland source and frothed down through a deep red channel, flowing toward the desert. Fern and monkey flowers grew along the cliffs of the gorge, and below where the creek straightened out, the water slowing its rush, cottonwoods and sycamore grew in a close tangle.

They sat on the rise, listening, watching, Shell leaning both hands on his pommel. After a time it came—the unmistakable sound of a horse nickering near the river.

Earl turned his face to Shell, eyes bright, eager.

"Well?"

"Reckon the horses could use a drink," Shell said, kneeing his black down the long bluff.

The wind was dry, smelling of water. The cottonwoods turned their leaves before it, flashing silver. The horse below nickered again.

20.

Shelter wound his horse through the cotton-woods. The shadows from the low sun flickered across the ground. The birds sang in the treetops, and down closer to the water, a frog grumped in the willows.

His horse moved silently across the sandy bottom; he carried his Colt in his hand, cocked and ready as his blue eyes searched the stand of trees. He paused, listening again. Earl was on his right, slightly behind him. Impatiently he watched Shelter.

It came muffled but distinctly—the sound of a horse blowing, shifting its feet so that the saddle creaked, and Shell nudged his horse forward, weaving through the trees.

The clouds beyond the gorge were tinted purple now, the shadows thickening as Shell and Earl Bentley came suddenly upon the clearing.

Alicia stood there, pretty if exhausted. Near her lay a dead horse. A second pony, shaky on its feet stood there eyeing them miserably.

And on a fallen log, Major Twyner.

Shelter heard Earl's gun cock and he spun toward Bentley. "He's mine," Shell said, and Earl saw a determination in those blue-gray eyes which he did not want to challenge.

"All right."

Slowly they rode into the clearing. The Major simply watched them, his face drawn, sallow. Beside him on the cottonwood log sat a pistol. Alicia watched patiently as Shelter swung down, followed by Earl Bentley.

"Game's up, Major," Shelter told him.

"Yes. I guess it is." Twyner seemed to have lost all of his fight. Perhaps he could see now that there was no way it could end differently.

"Are you going to shoot me?" Twyner asked. "Or are you going to let that scum do it?" he nodded toward Earl who flinched angrily.

"No need for you to get shot." Shelter dropped the reins to his horse and took another step. Twyner's eyes were glazed, his jaw slack. He was thinking of something and seemed not to hear Shell.

"We're a long way from Georgia, Captain."

"Yes, sir, we are."

"A lifetime away." Twyner added softly, "I wasn't ready to die."

"No need to," Shell said. "Come back to Pueblo with me—that's all I want. Stand trial for the Butterfield hold ups."

"That would be punishment enough?"

"It would satisfy me," Shell told him honestly. The Major slowly shook his head, lifting his eyes to Shell. "You realize how old I would be when I got out?"

"Maybe they'd go light on you."

"In Colorado!" The Major laughed loud and long, throwing back his head. "There were drivers killed during those holdups."

"I guess you'd have to answer to that."

"The hell!"

"It's the only way, sir."

"No." He shook his head, a little wearily it seemed. "It's not the only way." Then his hand flickered toward the Colt beside him and Shell fired twice.

The Major got to his feet, blood flowing from his shoulder and upper chest. He took a step toward Shell, still raising that gun and Shell fired again. The Major nodded, half-smiled and slumped to the earth, blood staining the earth beneath him, his Colt a few feet away, still cocked.

"He got what he wanted," Earl said. "Now I mean to do the same."

Shell turned his head just slightly, and he

could see Earl's gun trained on him. "Drop it, Shelter."

"All right."

His Colt thudded to the ground and Earl kicked it away. "Get over by the lady," Earl said. When Shelter had gone to where Alicia stood waiting, Earl crossed the clearing, going to the dead horse.

He found what he was looking for, and stood, gold sack in his hand.

"Shelter . . . I'm going to have to kill you," Earl said. If there was any genuine regret in his words, it was awful thin.

"Why? You got the gold."

"I don't want a man like you on my trail."

"I won't follow you, Earl."

"I could never be sure, could I?" Earl had worked his way around the clearing. Now he was at his horse, and he tossed the sack over his roll, tying it with one hand as the other kept his pistol trained on Shell.

"I never wanted the gold, Earl. I still don't," Shell told him. "It was only Twyner and Plum— you know that."

"I'd like to believe it," Earl said uncertainly. "Damned if I don't like you, Shell. No . . . I respect you."

"I won't be coming, Earl," Shell said evenly.

Earl frowned, eased his pony forward some and took the reins to Shell's black horse. Slowly, with a grin he put his pistol away.

"Damned if I don't believe you. It might cost me, but I believe you, Shelter." Then he let out a whoop and put the heels to his horse, whistling a tune as he rode out of the clearing.

Shell watched him go, Alicia next to him. They watched until there was nothing more to see, Earl's whistling still hanging in the air.

"Well," Alicia said, "and where does that leave us?"

"Together." His eyes swept her dark, handsome body and he added. "That suits me."

She smiled, fully and followed him as he walked to the foundered horse Earl had left behind. "Can we ride him?" she asked.

"Some, maybe. After a while. For now, let's start walking if you've got it in you."

"Walking where?" Alicia asked, her dark eyes wide, teasing.

"Anywhere at all where there's plenty of people, a bath and a bed. A bath most of all—I can't think of a thing better in this world right now."

Slowly they climbed out of the gorge, leading the horse behind them. They were not far from Bowie—he would finally see it, it seemed.

Dusk was a brilliant display of orange upon the desert, crimson and purple on the high, tattered clouds. The wind swept over them as they stopped atop a low ridge, gazing southward. Shell pointed out Earl to her.

He was a mile away, moving due south, deeper into Mexico. He seemed to pause and look back. Perhaps he saw them, though it seemed unlikely. They saw Earl lift his hat and wave it.

And at that moment they saw twenty horsemen appear from the dunes. Thumb's bare chested braves. They saw Earl start to run his horses, heard a shot and then another. And then there was nothing to see. Night was closing in around them and Shell shook his head.

"He had it for a time at least," he said. "Come on, let's get walking. With luck we'll make Bowie by suppertime. And I mean to have that bath. With plenty of hot water . . . maybe they'll have one of those brushes I can scrub my back with."

"And what makes you think you'll need a brush to get your back scrubbed?" Alicia asked, her smile again breaking free, her eyes dancing in the twilight.

Shell did not answer. Instead he turned to the horse, tightening the cinch.

"I think the horse can stand it. Let's ride a ways."

She looked worriedly down the backtrail. "All right," she replied, "if you think it's safer."

"Safer?" Shell swung into the saddle. "What I think is that it's *faster*." He grinned and stuck out a hand, helping her up behind him. Then he kneed the horse across the desert toward the silhouette of Fort Bowie, the dark-eyed girl clinging tightly to him.

THE SURVIVALIST SERIES
by Jerry Ahern